720

More praise for Julie Smith
and DEATH TURNS A TRICK

"A lively romp of a novel which heralds an interesting new detective personality . . . Smith shows an Agatha Christie-like capacity for making much ado about clues, concocting straw hypotheses, and surprising us, in the end. . . . Smith's crisp storytelling, her easy knowledge of local practices, and her likable, unpredictable heroine will make readers look forward to more of sleuth Schwartz's adventures."
San Francisco Chronicle

"The book gives readers an unusual look at San Francisco and introduces them to a delightfully modern sleuth."
Minneapolis Tribune

"The first-person narration has considerable charm, and the book leaves me eager for future adventures."
Ellery Queen

"Rebecca's lively first-person narration brands her a new detective to watch."
Wilson Library Bulletin

"Funny and witty, with a clever, outspoken heroine."
Library Journal

DEATH TURNS A TRICK

Julie Smith

IVY BOOKS • NEW YORK

Ivy Books
Published by Ballantine Books
Copyright © 1982 by Julie Smith

Library of Congress Catalog Card Number: 82-60308

ISBN 0-8041-0856-0

Manufactured in the United States of America

First Ballantine Books Edition: April 1992

THIS BOOK IS FOR MY PARENTS, with gratitude for invaluable assistance with motivation and character development; also for many clues, a few red herrings, and the occasional solution.

SPECIAL THANKS TO FIVE PEOPLE whose good advice helped shape this book: Inspector Dave Toschi, Betsy Petersen, Jon Carroll, Mary Jean Haley, and Mickey Friedman.

CHAPTER 1

The argument was getting loud, so I played loud to drown it out. I was looking at the keyboard, I guess, or maybe staring into space, I don't know which. Anyway, I didn't see two uniformed cops come in the door with guns drawn. I just heard a hush and then some screams. That made me look up. I saw them and stopped playing. People in the foyer were crowding back toward the stairs. Elena Mooney was backing toward the fireplace.

"Awright, everybody quiet," said one of the cops. "This is a raid." Those very words.

It's funny how you react in a situation like that. I should have been terrified. I should have had visions of lurid headlines: "Lawyer Caught in Bordello Raid." I should have despaired of my Martindale-Hubbell rating and started planning how I was going to explain to my mother. But I didn't. I was looking down the barrel of a gun and hearing someone say "This is a raid"—a thing I'd done a million times in movie theaters. I gripped the piano so I wouldn't holler, "Cheezit, the cops!"

Then the lights went out. I don't mean I fainted; I mean it got dark. A hand closed over my forearm, jerked me to my feet and started pulling. People started screaming again, and one of the cops fired. I didn't know if anybody was hit or not, but the reality of the situation dawned on me and I offered whoever was pulling me no resistance. We bumped into a lot of people getting through the saloon room, but it

1

took about two seconds, I guess. I vaguely heard things like "Don't panic" and "Be quiet," which I suppose came from the cops, and I heard two more shots and a lot more screaming.

My rescuer pulled the kitchen door open and me through it. The kitchen window had café curtains, and there was a little light from outside, enough to see that I was with Elena. She dropped my arm, grabbed a flashlight from the top of the refrigerator, and opened a door that I imagined led to a pantry. But I was wrong. Elena shone the light on steps descending to a basement.

She gestured for me to go first, then followed, locking the door behind us. There was a tiny landing at the bottom of the stairway and, on the right, a doorway to the basement itself. You couldn't see into it from the stairs.

When I got to the landing, I waited for Elena to join me with the light, but she turned it off as soon as she got there. I noticed a faint glow coming from the doorway to the basement. Elena put a finger to her lips and squeezed past me into the room. I followed.

The room was unfinished, but the plasterboard was painted. The light came from a silver candelabrum on the floor, with all its black candles lighted. Attached to two beams on the far wall were manacles at ankle and shoulder level. Some scary-looking hoists and pulleys hung from ceiling beams, but I can't say I was in a mood to examine them too closely. In fact, it's a miracle I noticed them at all, considering what else was in the room—a brass bed with a naked man lying face up, spread-eagled on it.

His wrists were tied to the headboard and his ankles to the footboards. Even without his customary conservative suit, I recognized him. He was State Senator Calvin Handley. That same week I'd seen him on TV holding a press conference about the bill he'd just introduced to legalize prostitution. At least he wasn't a hypocrite.

Elena still had her finger to her lips for his benefit. She

removed it and started untying his wrists. "Rebecca, get his ankles," she whispered.

She spoke to the client, without addressing him as "Senator"—on the off chance, I suppose, that I wouldn't recognize him. "There's been some trouble. The cops are here, but the door's locked and we'll have time to get you out of here. Where are your clothes?"

"I think Kandi forgot to bring them down. We came down the usual way."

"Damn her!" Elena finished freeing the senator's hands, and he sat up and rubbed them. She looked in an armoire at the front of the room. "She forgot, all right. You'll have to wear this."

She picked up something black from a low chair. In the chair underneath the black garment were a pair of handcuffs and a square of black fabric fashioned into a blindfold. I figured it must be quite a trick to negotiate those stairs coming down "the usual way," but *chacun a son goût*. Consenting adults and all that.

I finished with the senatorial ankle bonds, and the lawmaker slipped the black garment on. It was a floor-length robe with full sleeves and a hood, perfectly decent but damn-all odd.

"Shoes?" asked Elena. The senator shook his head. "Okay, come on. You too, Rebecca."

She pushed aside the armoire, revealing a crude passageway—a tunnel, really. She gave me the flashlight and fished a key from her bodice. As she handed it over, I could see that her hand was shaking. "Listen, both of you," she whispered. "Shots were fired up there. For all I know, someone may be dead or hurt. This is my house and I can't leave. Rebecca, this is . . . Joe. I'm depending on you to get him to his car. Then go home, change into street clothes, and get back here. We'll be needing you. The door at the end of the tunnel is padlocked, and this is the key. My car is parked almost dead against the door. It's unlocked and the keys are in it. Take the padlock with you; we may need to use the tunnel again tonight. Just get the sen—get Joe out of here. I'll wait five minutes after I hear the car drive off before I go back up. Good luck.'' She squeezed my hand.

We had to bend nearly double in the tunnel. I went first with the light, the senator following with a hand on each of my hips. I felt this was not completely necessary, but I put up with it. It was the least of my problems at the moment. I cursed whatever insanity had made me comply with Elena's request, and I cursed Elena for making it sound so safe.

She hadn't exactly lied. It was true no one was turning tricks at the party. But leaving out a naked senator in the basement was a rather serious sin of omission, if you ask me.

Senator *alter kocker* took his hands off me long enough to hold the light while I unlocked the door. Elena's Mustang was parked close, all right, but not close enough to avoid stepping in a mud puddle getting in. Since I had on sandals and the senator was barefoot, it was deuced inconvenient.

The Mustang snorted a couple of times, then laid back its ears and reared. We were in a lane that led to Broderick Street.

''Where's your car?'' I asked as we reached the street.

''Oh my God. I've got to go back—I haven't got my keys.''

''Keys, hell. You can't go back. I'll take you home.''

''But my money! My ID! They'll find it. I've got to get it. Turn around.''

''No.''

''I said turn around.''

''Look,'' I said. ''The cops don't care about johns. They'll probably just return your things discreetly. It'll be embarrassing, but nothing compared to being caught traipsing around a bordello in that outfit.''

''Goddammit, turn around.''

A citizen likes to think her elected officials have at least a minimal amount of brains in their tiny heads, whatever their sexual proclivities. But this guy had fried eggs. I stopped trying to reason with him. I could see he wasn't used to taking orders, except maybe from Kandi when they played amusing games, so I stopped being firm. I just drove, more or less in the direction of my apartment, and carefully, because of the rain.

He was quiet for a minute or two, so I tried again as we turned onto Fillmore Street. This time I tried to sound helpful and cheerful like a secretary or a wife, someone he could identify with. "Where can I drop you off?"

"Goddammit, young woman, take me back!" he shouted.

"You're out of your senatorial head!" I shouted back. "Where the hell do you live?"

He reached over and grabbed the wheel. I lost control and we skidded to the right, tires squealing like seagulls. I jerked the wheel back in time to avoid plowing into a parked car, and slammed on the brakes. But I overcompensated and winged the parked car with the rear end of the Mustang. I heard a siren even as I felt the bump, and I looked in the mirror. The red light of a police car was half a block away.

Before I could get my bearings, that fruitcake of a senator had his door open and his bare feet on Fillmore Street. Without so much as a "thanks for the lift," he rounded the car we'd hit, stepped up on the sidewalk, and took off running, with that silly black robe billowing behind him. In that context, he looked like just another San Francisco freak, only they don't usually have a fine head of silvery hair. I leaned over and shut the passenger door, hoping the cops hadn't seen him. They pulled up as he turned the corner.

The cop who got out of the patrol car had a fine silky mustache, and the rest of him looked okay, too. "Are you all right, ma'am?" he asked.

"I think so. I skidded in the rain and pulled too far back."

"Let's see your driver's license."

"I—uh—had an emergency. I don't have it."

"You've got your keys. They must have been in your purse with your license."

"No, they were already in the car."

"What's your name?"

"Rebecca Schwartz."

"You been drinking, Miss Schwartz?"

"A little. That's not why I hit the car, though. I skidded."

"How about parking the car over there on the curb, Miss Schwartz? I'll be with you in a minute."

I don't do my best parking jobs in situations of stress, but I don't think the cop noticed. He was doing something with his partner in the patrol car.

He joined me in a minute. "You got any ID at all?"

"I told you I didn't."

"We just ran this car through the computer. It's registered to an Elena Mooney."

"I know. I borrowed it from her."

"Does she know you've got it?"

"Certainly."

"Miss Schwartz, I'm going to have to ask you to take a roadside sobriety test. Would you mind just stretching your arms out horizontally? Good. Okay now, put your head back a little, close your eyes, and touch your nose with the tip of your index finger."

"Left or right?"

"Both. Three times."

I never have been good at silly games. I hit my nose three out of six times, and that's as well as I can do cold sober. I know, because I've tried it a million times since. But I don't have to tell you the attractive cop wouldn't believe it was just a personal idiosyncrasy. I have to say he was nice about the whole thing, though. He seemed almost apologetic: "I hate to ask you on a night like this, but do you think you can walk a straight line, toe-to-heel?"

"I'll get wet."

"I'm sorry, ma'am." He was really nice, that fellow, especially considering I wasn't looking any too respectable.

The rain pelted into my cleavage as I got out of the car. I got up on the sidewalk, put one shoe in front of the other, and kept on doing it until the cop told me to stop. I wanted to go on, because I knew that line would straighten up as

soon as I got the hang of it, but the cop wasn't convinced.
I'd meandered pretty far off course.

"I'm afraid that emergency of yours is going to have to
wait, Miss Schwartz. You've just had an accident in a car
that's not yours, and you got no driver's license and no ID,
and you can't pass your sobriety test. And the car's got 200
dollars' worth of traffic warrants on it."

"But . . ."

"I don't think you'd better drive the Mustang. Just lock it,
please, and get in the backseat of the patrol car."

"Wait a minute. I can explain what I'm doing with the
car."

"All the explaining in the world's not going to convince
me you're sober."

So I locked the Mustang while they inspected the parked
car for damage. Then we sat in the patrol car, the cop with
the mustache and me, while his partner made out an accident
report. I never did figure out why that had to be done at the
scene instead of at the Hall, but it did give me time to pour
out my story.

I said I'd been to a costume party—which I had hoped
might explain my get-up—and that a friend had been suddenly taken ill. I was driving him to the hospital when I hit
the parked car.

"So where is he now?"

"He got frightened when I hit the car and ran away."

"How sick was he?"

I lowered my eyes. "I don't know. He was acting very
strangely. I think he was having some sort of nervous attack."

The cop came to the conclusion I wanted him to. He raised
an eyebrow. "Were there drugs at that party, Miss
Schwartz?"

I said there were, and he didn't ask any more questions.

On the way to the Hall, I assessed the situation. I was
dressed like a hooker, so they probably thought I was one in
spite of my lame little explanation; no one has costume par-

ties three weeks after Halloween. So there was no use protesting that I was a lawyer without an ID to back it up. It wouldn't do any good anyway, since they thought I was drunk.

I figured Elena and the others would be at the Hall. We could straighten out the ownership of the car and maybe establish my identification. Then we could call my partner to get us out.

But I wondered if she could. It might just be that Rebecca Schwartz, Jewish feminist lawyer, was about to spend a night in jail. I prayed I would pass my breathalyzer test. And when I got done praying, I mused on the dark and sinister forces that had gotten me into the backseat of a patrol car.

CHAPTER 2

They were dark forces inside my skull, of course. I remembered the time my mother turned on the cold tap and threw me in the shower with all my clothes on, just because, at the age of nine, I decided not to be a concert pianist. I'm not saying there wasn't provocation; I did come to the decision in the middle of a music lesson, and I did emphasize it by tearing up some sheet music and hurling a metronome. But it made a big impression on me. Maybe that's why I agreed to Elena Mooney's request—to get back at my mom. My shrink has since expressed the opinion that this was so.

But there could have been other reasons. Perfectly sensible reasons.

For one thing, I have led a dull life. I was twenty-eight at the time, and I had never done anything more exciting than make good grades and grow up to be a feminist Jewish lawyer. I never hitchhiked around Europe with nobody but my lover and nothing but my backpack. I never so much as spent a summer on a kibbutz.

I am not sure why, except that I am conservative by nature. I dislike change and am afraid to take chances; if I played poker, which I do not, I'd probably fold three kings unless I had a pair of aces to go with them. I grew up in Marin County, California, crossed the San Francisco Bay to go to law school in Berkeley, and crossed it again to practice in San Francisco. I come from a middle-class liberal Jewish family, and my politics and values don't deviate a whit from what I was taught as a child, except maybe in the areas of drugs and sex—I probably have a more contemporary approach to these than my parents.

Basically, I am the kind of girl that mothers wish their sons would marry. But nobody's son did, and anyway I couldn't be bothered. I was too busy living up to my *father*'s ambition for me. Or what I imagined it to be. He always said, "Be a doctor, Rebecca. There's no money in law," but anybody could see he was joking. When I was a little girl, he used to take me to watch him in court, and when I was a teenager, he'd discuss his cases with me. What did I know from doctors? I had a lawyer for a role model.

Now if you had led this kind of life and someone came along and said, "Listen, how would you like to play the piano in a whorehouse for just one night—you'll be among friends; nothing can happen," wouldn't you do it? Especially if it were a feminist bordello? It wouldn't have to be a case of getting back at your mom.

Another thing: Elena needed me. I should turn down a friend who needs a favor just because I'm too good to hang around a bordello? What kind of sisterhood is that?

I should explain about Elena. She is a prostitute, and she's also very close to being a madam, only she isn't quite because this is a co-op bordello we're talking about. It's co-op because ostensibly everyone has an equal say in decision-making and the money is split among the members, but Elena is actually the brains and the driving force of the thing. She'd be a madam in the old-fashioned sense if she weren't political.

I got to know her when she got busted and Jeannette von Phister asked me to take her case. Despite certain reservations I have about prostitution as a feminist issue ("horizontal hostility," Jeannette calls it), I was already on the legal staff of HYENA, the "loose women's organization" Jeannette had founded. As you no doubt know, HYENA is an acronym for "Head Your Ethics toward a New Age," and its ultimate goal is to get prostitution legalized.

By making it a feminist issue, they've managed to acquire a certain amount of clout, and they're quite colorful, so they get a lot of publicity. When I agreed to work for them, it may be that somewhere in my subconscious, I knew some of the publicity was bound to rub off on their lawyer. As a matter of fact, it did when I became Elena's lawyer.

Elena (née Eileen, I'll bet anything, but I've never had the nerve to ask) had been running this co-op feminist bordello for about six months. She had brains, but not a lot of experience. I think she probably didn't look carefully enough into the matter of police payoffs, but that's a fine thing for her lawyer to say, so pretend you didn't hear it. Anyway, she and her three partners got busted, and Jeannette called me to defend them.

The case made quite a splash. Elena ran a pretty classy house, and there were whispers of influential names in a certain address book found there. Also, HYENA did a lot of hollering about harassment; Jeanette and I held a press conference at which we berated the police department for wasting its time on consensual transactions between adults. I declared that my clients were the victims of a hypocritical society that kept wages for women low and yet persecuted them when they were forced into a life of prostitution, all the while winking at the part their clients played in the transaction. Anyway, my pronouncements led to appearances on talk shows, but probably had nothing to do with the fact that Elena and the others got probation. It was a first offense for all of them.

Elena and I got quite friendly, though. I liked her. She had a kind of unflappable earthiness that I suppose grew out of being one of six children in a poor family. She also had a good sense of humor, which probably had the same roots. Being the uptight, middle-class spinster I am, I wished she'd give up her life of crime and go back to school, but you can't run other people's lives for them.

When the case was over, we had lunch together a lot and I became conversant with curious and intimate details of a prostitute's life. But nothing hard on the stomach, you understand. Being Irish, Elena is a born raconteuse, and she can make life in a bordello sound like a Restoration comedy.

Sitting over crab salad and white wine in my gray flannel blazer and Cacharel blouse, I felt pretty naive as she spun tales about a world of crystal chandeliers and high-heeled sandals. A world where indulgence of personal vanity was not only not condemned but was actually applauded. I loved getting a peek at it. And there was a part of me that was attracted to it.

It must have been plain to Elena that drab, workaday Rebecca had certain fantasies not altogether suitable for a Jewish feminist lawyer, because first she sent me tickets to the Strumpets' Strut, an annual fund-raising ball HYENA holds at Halloween. Then in that atmosphere of feathers and sequins, she broke the news that she was back in business and invited me to tour her new place.

I wasn't her mother or her probation officer, and I didn't figure it was my place to lecture. Clearly, the civil thing to do was accept the invitation, admire her bordello, and do everything I could for her the next time she got busted.

We made a date for the following Saturday—in the morning, so she could open at noon as usual.

CHAPTER 3

We got to the Hall of Justice at 12:45, and I was arrested for suspicion of driving with intoxication. It was an ignominious moment for the Schwartz family.

The cops took me to the traffic bureau, which is a big room with a lot of desks and typewriters like a business office. I asked if I could call Elena.

"Sure, but first let's do your sobriety test. Blood, breath, or urine?"

"Breath," I said.

Then they gave me some time to myself. I tried to muster some positive thoughts about passing the test and getting out of there, but it was no good. My mind replayed the events that led to my being there, starting that Saturday a few weeks before, the day of my first visit to a bordello.

Elena's house was in Pacific Heights, but if you think I'm going to pin it down better than that, you're much mistaken. Client-attorney privilege.

It was a gracious example of the style known as Queen Anne Victorian, painted white with dark blue and gold trim. Dignified as you please.

Elena answered the door in jeans, but stepped quickly aside so I could get the full effect. The floor of the foyer was bare, but the staircase, which was eight or ten feet away, was carpeted in red. The walls of the foyer and the one that led up the staircase were covered in honest-to-God red-flocked whorehouse wallpaper. An old-fashioned oak coatrack was the only furniture in the foyer, and there was a chandelier of ruby glass with crystal prisms suspended from it.

"My God!" I said. "It's the Platonic cathouse."

"Not exactly the word I'd choose under the circumstances," said Elena.

"It's stunning."

She nodded. "No cliché overlooked. Except maybe a bead curtain. But the only place for it was the kitchen doorway, and I couldn't take the chance of some john wandering into make himself a toasted cheese sandwich."

She led me into the living room, which had a fireplace on the far side with the obligatory painting of a nude woman hung above it. Not a bad one, either. She was lying on her side on a brass bed, and she wasn't actually nude. She wore boots.

There was a rose satin loveseat with fringe around the bottom, and there was another of carved mahogany and wine-colored velvet. Chairs that matched the mahogany loveseat were covered in rose velvet (the kind that looks antique, but isn't). Naturally, Elena hadn't forgotten a crystal chandelier.

Toward the back of the room on the left, there was a conversational grouping of Victorian chairs and tables. On the right was a grand piano covered with a very fine old piano shawl. More naked ladies dotted the walls, with beauty spots dotting their faces and fannies.

"Very cozy," I said.

"Gaudy as hell," said Elena. "But homey. That's what the clutter's for. It's got to seem like a fantasy world, only not intimidating. And you have to make sure there's plenty of room to move around. See, you can dance in the foyer or in this bare space between the double parlors."

"It's perfect," I said. "Ever think of going into the decorating business?"

She laughed. "When I retire."

"You scofflaw."

"Come on, let me show you the upstairs. There's nothing else down here but the kitchen, and we'll have some tea there afterwards."

I won't describe Elena's bedroom, because I am trying to give you a glimpse of the demimonde and it wouldn't be relevant. So you won't be disoriented, though, I'll tell you it was one of four bedrooms upstairs. The other three were for tricks.

The red carpet from the stairway snaked down the hall and into two of them. These two were furnished with marble-topped tables, gilt mirrors, and carved mahogany beds with red velvet covers.

The third had only one piece of furniture: the biggest waterbed I've ever seen. And every inch of wall and ceiling was mirrored. "Not very Victorian," I observed.

"No," said Elena. "There's no accounting for taste. It's our most popular offering."

She led me back to the kitchen, which was much like any old kitchen except that it was big enough to get a fair-sized table into. I sat down as Elena made tea and English muffins.

"This is the only room I can really call my own, besides my bedroom," she said. "It's rather awful living here, really, but somebody has to—we couldn't just leave the place locked up except during working hours."

Watching Elena move about the kitchen in her jeans, I could imagine she found living at the bordello "rather awful." She had glossy chestnut hair and fine heavy brows, which she was smart enough not to pluck. You'd never have guessed she was a hooker if it weren't for her mandarin manicure.

It occurred to me that while I knew all about her life with the rollicking Chicago family, I didn't know how she'd made the transition to feminist prostitute. I'd met a lot of

HYENA members, and they all had similar stories; they had been secretaries or file clerks who turned to prostitution the first time someone offered them money for sex. They became feminists when the women's movement made the point that it's easier for men to make money than it is for women.

But Elena seemed more intelligent and better educated than the other hookers I knew. She sat down at the table with a pot of tea and the buttered muffins.

"Elena," I said, "You've never told me how you, uh . . ."

"Fell from grace?" She poured tea.

"Well, yes."

"Learned my trade in college, just like you did." She laughed. "It was the University of Chicago. History department. It happened in my sophomore year when I was going to class and working full-time as a waitress. I was beat to hell, which wasn't that hard to spot—I'd lost about ten pounds and I always seemed to have circles under my eyes. So one of my professors took a fancy to me and let me in on an easier way."

"A man?"

"No. A woman. She'd worked her way through graduate school by turning tricks."

"Oh, come on."

Elena shrugged. "Well, I can't prove it, but she did seem to know what she was doing. She said she knew a man who'd been wanting to meet me. He was willing to pay a hundred dollars, but the deal was, I had to give fifty back to the teacher."

"A *history* professor?"

"I was a bit shocked myself, but I've since learned that's the way these things are done. Pretty soon I was making twice what I made at the waitress job for only a few hours' work a week."

"So did you finish school?"

"No. I got through my junior year, but by that time I was so successful, I thought: what's the point of school if I can make this kind of money without an education? So I decided to try the big-time in San Francisco. I worked bars for a while and did okay, then I got to know a few of my colleagues. Jeannette formed HYENA, and I liked the approach. You know—prostitution as a profession, with a union and everything. Then Stacy and Renee and Hilary and I decided to set up the co-op."

"Do you ever regret not getting your degree?"

"I can always go back and get it if I want to. But, look, I know what you're getting at. I'm not dumb, and I have a talent for decorating, as you pointed out. I could probably do other things, right? So why be a prostitute when I have a choice?"

"Well?"

" I don't know. I try not to think about it too much. It probably has to do partly with manipulating people, playing roles, working out fantasies. But more than that, it's a fear of failure at something else—and fear of being poor again. This is something I'm good at, and a good way to make money, so I'm not ready to give it up yet.

"But you know, don't you, that every prostitute dreams of the day she can retire? I'll tell you something—I probably *will* be a decorator someday. Or do something in that field—maybe a nice little antique store. Somebody who hasn't been poor, though, I can't figure out why they'd do this. We've got a part-timer named Kandi who comes from a good family; she could have done anything."

Elena shrugged. "Maybe she's just a greedy, manipulative, lazy little bitch. And maybe I am, too."

On the way out, I stopped to admire the piano shawl a little more carefully, and my fingers went automatically to the keys. I'd never have made a professional musician—Mom was dead wrong about that—but I have a good ear and I love a piano. Before I stopped to think, I sat down on the old-fashioned stool and started banging out "Maple Leaf Rag."

Don't ask me why that tune came into my head—maybe because it was exactly right for the setting.

Elena looked at me as if I'd pulled a family of rabbits out of my bra.

CHAPTER 4

A breathalyzer works like this: You breathe into the mouth-piece of a small machine and your breath is captured in a cylinder and then run through some sort of chemical solution. You have to do it twice, and it takes less than 15 minutes for both tests.

Nothing to it. I say this because I passed.

"Am I still under arrest?" I asked when I got the good news.

"Not for drunk driving," said the cop with the mustache. "But we'd better talk with the owner of the Mustang. Can you get her for us?"

"Sure." They didn't know all they'd have to do was go up to City Prison on the sixth floor to talk to her, and I didn't tell them. My plan was to call Elena's and then pretend I'd gotten a message she was at the Hall. That way maybe it would look like I'd left before the raid.

But Elena herself answered the phone.

I left Elena's, and not having so much as a tennis date for the afternoon, I went shopping for something to wear that night. I was just having dinner with Chris Nicholson, my law partner, and her long-time love, Larry Hughes, but there was going to be another guest—a friend of Larry's they thought I might like. Maybe I had in mind dolling myself up so irresistibly that he'd want to fall into my arms, but I don't think so, judging from what I brought home. I thinks it's more

19

likely that I was motivated by whatever quirk it is that makes me hungry for fresh fish after a visit to the aquarium. I'd just been to a bordello, remember.

I went to Magnarama at Stonestown, where, as you know, you can sometimes find astonishing bargains. I was pawing idly through a rack of shopworn blouses when my eye caught a metallic glint. I'm not much up on fabrics, but I think it was silver lamé. In about two seconds, I was in the dressing room tearing up my fingernails on the thing's thirty-or-so silver-covered buttons. It was a sort of jacket, made in a 1940s style. Shoulder pads, narrow waist, and a little flounce around the bottom. It had long, tight sleeves with eight or ten more of those pesky buttons and a prim, rounded collar that must have been a good eighteen inches long before it was attached, because you could have shot me through the heart without damaging the garment. It fit as sleekly as a leotard.

I am five-feet-five inches tall and weigh 125 pounds, which is not exactly fat, but it isn't going to get me any modeling contracts. I wouldn't say I have what novelists call a "copious bosom," but I don't think "generous" is going too far, and there's no question it's my best feature. This little silver number set it off to optimum advantage.

You won't believe what I found to go with it: a wraparound black satin skirt that only continued wrapping for a few inches down from the waist, so it looked like it was slit up to the wazoo, but it actually revealed a good deal more than a slit would have. Like most of my left leg. What there was of it fell to the calf, slick and shiny as a wetsuit.

The entire outfit cost me twenty-five dollars.

I don't know where drab, workaday Rebecca was that day, but whoever was impersonating her bought a pair of false eyelashes, a pair of sheer black nylons, and what my sister Mickey calls wicked-woman shoes—high-heeled, open-toed sandals.

Then she stole Rebecca's good gray Volvo from the parking lot, drove it to Rebecca's Telegraph Hill apartment, and let herself in as if she owned the place.

I am going to take time out to tell you what she found there, as I am very fond of my apartment, and you are going to be spending a lot of time there. The colors are stark, wintry ones. For warmth I have a grand piano, an enormous window with a great view and, underneath the window, the thing I love most in the world: a hundred-gallon saltwater aquarium. It teems with hermit crabs and fish in colors you wouldn't believe, and even shrimp. But the anemones— translucent, pink, and always reaching for something just outside their grasp—are my favorites.

Because the aquarium doesn't quite fill the space under the window, it's flanked by the fattest, most luxuriant asparagus ferns you ever saw, each like a green basketball on its white ceramic stand.

It's a beautiful, wonderful apartment, its sophistication marred only by a funny little Don Quixote sculpture on the coffee table—an incongruous, cornball item weighing about a ton. I'd bought it in Mexico with my ex-boyfriend, and I couldn't bring myself to get rid of it.

So that's what the stranger saw when she went into Rebecca's apartment that day. She walked right through to the bedroom, where she spent half an hour applying the eyelashes, cursing every minute, and then she slithered lamia-like into the rest of the caparison. Peering eagerly into Rebecca's mirror, she gazed upon none other than Rebecca Schwartz looking like a silly ass.

Having returned from whatever astral plane I'd been on, I looked in that mirror and hooted like a gibbon. When I'd finished making sport of myself, I peeled off the eyelashes, slithered lamia-like out of everything else, stepped into the shower, and washed that alter ego right out of my hair.

I wore a black sweater and a pair of violet corduroys to Chris and Larry's.

Chris met me at the door, looking about nine feet tall in a

yellow jumpsuit. Before you could say, "habeas corpus," she plunged right in: "You're gonna like this guy."

I didn't take it as bad news. I was wearing boring old corduroys, but I had got up the nerve to put on the wicked-woman shoes, and I was feeling pretty reckless. "Tell me more," I said.

Chris led me into the kitchen on the pretext of getting some wine. "He's Parker Phillips, who's just moved here from pigball," she said. "An architect."

Now of course I knew he hadn't moved from pigball, but I'm used to Chris. Since Larry's from Seattle, I deduced that was what she meant. Chris is a very good lawyer, but she gives the appearance of being scatterbrained because whenever she can't think of a word, she just substitutes a made-up one. "Pigball" was her latest.

"What's he look like?" I asked. I don't like to think I'm a female chauvinist pig, but I do set a certain store by a man's appearance.

"Very New England. Not a West Coast type at all. Six feet tall, smokes a pipe, light brown hair, good bones. Ready to meet him?"

Who was going to say no after that description?

Parker Phillips had a firm handshake and perfect manners to go with it. He also seemed a little on the shy side, a quality which I feel shows a person isn't unduly impressed with himself.

"Chris says you just moved to San Francisco," I said when Larry and Chris had faded discreetly into the kitchen.

"Yes. My marriage broke up last year, and I'd been wanting to get out of Seattle for months. So when I got a job offer here, I took it. It seemed like a good place to live, and anyway I already knew two people here—Larry and my sister Carol, who's a student at San Francisco State."

Then he asked me about my law practice, and I started to warm up to him. I like men who ask me about myself. That old high school advice—that you should talk to men about what they're interested in—is a good way to bore yourself silly.

I told Parker all about my star client. Then, as he still seemed interested, I told him about my bordello tour and regaled him with a few of Elena's stories. I even confessed my silly shopping trip. He was kind enough to admire my wicked-woman shoes and asked if they were good for dancing. I said I'd show him sometime.

Which I did, after dinner; we left early and went to a little place I know.

After we danced awhile, we talked some more and I learned several things of interest:

When he laughed, he used his whole face.

He played tennis.

He liked classical music.

His favorite movie was *King of Hearts*, which is only my third favorite, but that's close enough.

I was quite prepared to pack for an indefinite stay and run away with him if he asked me.

He didn't, so I invited him over to see my aquarium. It was a bold move, but I had on wicked-woman shoes.

I left the lights off, because the aquarium was lit, and so was the whole city of San Francisco on the other side of the window. We sipped brandy and smoked a joint. The anemones performed their endless, delicate, futile tentacle-dance. The hermit crabs were good for comic relief. San Francisco was lambent as the Emerald City. It was better than *King of Hearts*, so after a while I made popcorn. A while after that, we made love.

CHAPTER 5

Elena spoke before I could: "Rebecca, you poor baby, out on a night like this without your keys! Where are you calling from?"

"I'm at the Hall of Justice. Why aren't you?"

"I forgot you didn't know. It wasn't a raid after all. Just some sort of dumb practical joke arranged by some of the guests. The shots were blanks, thank God. But what are you doing at the Hall?"

"Trying to prove I didn't steal your car. Would you mind talking to the nice officer?"

I handed him the phone; he asked her some questions, and they negotiated. I was tired and I wanted to go home.

It was your basic fairytale evening, all right. But Parker and I were both mature adults with degrees from the well-known school of hard knocks. We didn't plight our troth on the spot. By mutual unspoken consent, we decided to exercise reasonable caution with each other. We went tidepooling the next day and had a liquid, romantic lunch at one of those roadside fish places down the Peninsula, but we didn't spend Sunday night together.

In fact, we didn't see each other again until the next weekend, when we went to a Buñuel movie. I was in love, but this is not unusual. My average (except for the two years I was with Gary Wildman) is four times a year, and the average length of the infatuation is three weeks. I keep seeing my lovers—usually about three to six months—but the edge is generally off after the first few dates, when I start finding fault. I didn't find any in Parker the night of the movie, though. He didn't whine at me about his broken heart, and he did laugh at my jokes. I remained in love and we made a third date.

The third Friday in November, the appointed day for our third date—and incidentally the longest day of my life—it started raining before I woke up and showed no signs of letting up for the next thirty-nine days and thirty-nine nights. I spent the morning calming a client whose impending divorce was threatening her reason and then popped over to Heshie's with Chris for a pastrami sandwich and a cream soda.

"I hear you're going out with pigball tonight," she said when we were settled. "Larry and I asked him to dinner and he confessed. Is he Mr. Right or not?"

"He seems pretty solid."

"God, Rebecca, you are the most conservative woman I've ever met. No wonder you're never in love for more than three weeks. How in hell did you ever manage to move in with Gary?"

"I wasn't nearly so cautious in those days. Besides, it was entirely his idea; he practically dragged me to his cave by the hair."

"You never really told me why it didn't work out."

"His decision to live with me was the last one he ever made while we were together."

"What are you talking about? I always thought you and Gary had the most egalitarian relationship of anyone I knew. Larry thought so, too."

"Yeah, so did I. It wasn't till much later that I realized I had a son instead of a lover. It was all very subtle, you see. Nobody is going to ask a feminist lawyer to cook his meals and do his laundry. He didn't want a mother for that stuff."

"So what do you mean?"

"He wanted to be told what to do: what courses to take,

whether to listen to classical music or rock—even, I kid you not, whether to have a spot of dalliance with someone else.''

"Oh Jesus.''

"I thought at the time we were merely discussing these things in a sharing, adult fashion, but I realized later that I was making all the decisions. And not only that; Gary had to be constantly reassured about his self-doubts and patted on the head and told what a good boy he was.''

"It couldn't have been that bad. If Gary wants a mother, what's he doing now with a twenty-two-year-old peach blossom?'' This was a bit of a sore spot, because Gary left me for said peach blossom.

"He outgrew me,'' I said. "You might be able to carry on a mother-son relationship forever, except that little boys grow up and rebel against their moms. It hit me pretty hard when he left me for Melissa, if you recall.''

Chris nodded.

"But now you have pigball.''

"Parker.'' I couldn't help smiling. "Yes. And I meant it when I said he seemed solid. I think he actually might be a man who's able to take care of himself.''

"What are you two doing tonight?''

"Oh, I don't know. Probably dinner and a movie. We'd better go back to the office so I won't miss his call.''

That was about the only reason for going back to the office that Friday, to tell the truth. I didn't have any appointments, so I planned to spend the afternoon doing research on some pending cases. But I could have done that any old time, and the longer I could put it off the better, in my opinion. The one thing I hate about law is poring over musty old law books.

While I pondered, weak and weary, the telephone rang. Thinking it was Parker, I didn't pick it up till the third ring, so as not to seem too eager. It was Elena Mooney.

"Rebecca, I'm in a hell of a fix. Have you ever heard of the FDOs?''

"No.''

"It stands for Friday Downtown Operators. They're a bunch of—oh, fifty or seventy-five young businessmen who meet for lunch every Friday just so they can invite whatever sweet young things they've had their eyes on. It's supposed to be an honor to get an invitation."

I believe I may have snorted, but Elena went on anyway. "Well, apparently a lot of them wanted to go to the Strumpets' Strut, but they couldn't get tickets, so they got it into their heads to have their own. They called Jeannette von Phister and asked if she knew of a bordello they could rent for it, and she set it up with me. The girls and I will be there as hostesses, but it's just a party—nobody's going to turn any tricks. They guys will all have dates anyway.

"The problem is, it's tonight and I had a wonderful black guy who wears an ice-cream suit all lined up to play piano, but he's sick. I know it's short notice, but do you think you could possibly . . ."

"Elena, I'd love to, but I have a date."

"For heaven's sake, bring him."

"Oh no, I couldn't. What if I ran into someone I knew?"

"For Christ's sake, it's just a party. You were at the Strumpets' Strut with every pimp and whore in San Francisco, and so were the chief of police and the sheriff. What's the difference?"

"That wasn't at a bordello."

"Look, I live there. All it is is a party at Elena Mooney's rather overdecorated Pacific Heights home. If no one's turning tricks, how's it a bordello?" She should have been a lawyer.

"They got you last time for 'keeping a disorderly house.' How do you know the cops won't raid it?"

"Uh uh. Anybody gets disorderly, he gets thrown out. And don't worry about the music. The fellow in the ice-cream suit comes in every weekend and people are always dancing. The place is soundproofed."

I couldn't see a single thing against it. If I bumped into some lawyer I knew, the incontrovertible fact was that he

was there too. Anyway, everybody knows I'm Elena's lawyer. What could be more natural than helping out a friend?
I told Elena I'd call Parker and call her back.

Parker jumped at it.

"There's just one thing," said Elena when I called back.
"Could you wear something sort of—uh—in keeping with
the occasion?"

I told her I had just the thing—my Magnarama outfit—and
arranged to come early so she could work on my hair and
face. Since the make-up session was bound to bore Parker,
he and I decided to come in separate cars.

It was still raining that night, and I had to wear a trench-
coat and boots. Once they were off, Elena breathed a sigh of
relief. "That'll do nicely," she said. "In twenty minutes you
won't recognize yourself."

I handed over my eyelashes, and she wrestled them on in
about two seconds. Next, she applied blue eye shadow and
a lot of rouge that followed the cheekbones exactly and didn't
look half-bad. I said I wanted a beauty mark, and she obliged
me—on the right cheek between the nose and mouth. She
fossicked in her bureau for the right shade of carmine lipstick
and let me apply it myself, a skill I learned in junior high.
From another drawer, she pulled the pièce de résistance—a
silver lamé turban, so help me. It covered every strand of my
Montgomery Street coiffure and, with the addition of a pair
of dangling silver earrings, transformed workaday Rebecca
into the expensive courtesan of my fantasies.

I didn't look like a streetwalker, you understand. Merely
a very high-class lady of uncertain reputation. I was pro-
foundly pleased with the effect.

Elena's own hair was pulled back from her face and piled
very high in front, but was left hanging loose in back. So-
phisticated, but not quite nice. She wore a slithery black
velvet number that was long on sleeves and short on skirt. In
fact, I learned that night that the miniskirt has never gone
out of style at fancy cathouses. I was the only one of us *filles*

de joie whose knees were covered, but then I had a slit to the wazoo, so what did it matter?

Elena took me to the kitchen for a spot of sherry before the guests arrived. The other hostesses were gathered round the table, drinking only tea and soft drinks. Though they were passing a joint around, they were pros and didn't want to smell like alcohol. Hilary, Renée, and Stacy, the other members of the co-op, were also my clients, so we knew each other from jail. I was introduced to Kandi, whose last name could have been Floss or Apple or Kane with no suspension of disbelief required. If you'd told me she'd made it up and was really Stephanie or Betsy or Suzy Q, I wouldn't have had any. She was a sugarplum that walked like a woman. Sensuous as homemade fudge, airy as cotton candy, and cloying as divinity. She wasn't any of those, though: she was a meringue. (This is not a sexist remark, merely an observation: I am a cinnamon heart, Parker is English toffee, former President Carter is a Mr. Goodbar, Richard Nixon is a licorice whip, Pat Nixon is a frosting rose from a birthday cake. I could go on forever.)

Kandi had frilly blond hair and a figure that bounced with self-congratulation. But I don't have to describe her too much because you know her: think of the homecoming queen at your high school, and there you have it. Half all-American girl, half budding starlet, and so radiant your eyes hurt to look at her. Only Kandi had passed out of the girl stage and the budding stage, and had flowered into a confectioner's idea of a prostitute. She wore an apricot chiffon dress, long-sleeved and form-fitting, with a furbelow of a skirt like skaters wear. Neckline, cuffs, and hem were fluffy with tiny, downy apricot feathers.

As for Hilary, Renée, and Stacy, if they'd come to court in the outfits they had on, they'd have been spending that November in the pokey. Hilary had on a nurse's uniform, thigh-high with white sequins all over.

Renée—a large, fortyish woman—wore a scarlet, plunging blouse of some shiny material, a wide belt, and a tight black skirt that hugged her opulent fanny and fell nearly to her knees, but not quite.

Stacy, scarcely five feet tall and flat as a boy, wore a dress of white dotted swiss trimmed with a Peter Pan collar and tied in the back with an old-fashioned perky sash. She had braided her hair, tied it with pink ribbons, and painted freckles across her nose.

I had to admire Elena. She had certainly provided for every fantasy, from Kandi the prom queen to Renée the storybook whore. Even an exotic woman of mystery. Me.

My musical plan for the evening was to intersperse Scott Joplin with old-timey whorehouse blues and, since the guests would have dates and so would I, a few romantic favorites: "These Foolish Things," "As Time Goes By," that sort of thing. But Scott Joplin first, to set a rollicking mood.

Every light in the place was controlled by a dimmer, and Elena had set them low to produce a rosy glow. As I sat down at the piano stool, Renée walked by and made me think of the Place Pigalle, so I played "Milord" instead of "Maple Leaf Rag." It upset my plan, but it was perfect guest-welcoming music.

The FDOs and their dates arrived in breathless groups of twos and fours, practically shaking themselves like wet birds. They lost no time in handing their raingear to the genial hostesses and getting into the party spirit. I tried to give each new group what I believe is called a broad wink.

They were dressed for a party, those people, the men in coats and ties and the women in silk dresses, showing lots of skin.

For a while, Elena was kept busy answering the door, while the other four served champagne, which is the only appropriate drink for a bordello. Every time Kandi swept by, she left a little cloud of tiny feathers in her wake, causing me to sneeze and miss an occasional note. But that, and the fact that working the pedals made it nearly impossible to preserve any semblance of decency—what with the slit in my skirt—were my only hardships. Every now and then, someone brought me a glass of champagne, so I was in a wonderful mood by the time Parker arrived.

It was time for a break, so I took one. "Irma La Douce, I presume," he said by way of greeting.

I got up and showed off. "Like my outfit?"

"What there is of it."

"Am I fascinating?" I gave it a hard "c."

"Scintillating," he said, doing the same. "You look like a mill—I mean, at least three or four hundred."

I put a hand on my hip and thrust my chest out. "I could give you a deal."

"Rebecca!" said a female voice. It was Stacy, holding a silver tray loaded with full champagne glasses. "What is this—amateur hour?"

"Stacy," I said, "this is Parker. My date."

She gave us champagne and floated away. "One of your clients?" asked Parker.

"Uh huh. You can tell the whores by the length of their skirts."

Parker looked horrified. "What's the big deal?" I asked. "We were all wearing miniskirts a few—" I stopped because he was no longer listening. Apparently, the big deal wasn't anything I said. It was something his eyes were following, something on the other side of the room. I looked, but all I saw was a knot of people taking drinks from a tray Kandi was holding.

CHAPTER 6

The cops offered Elena a terrific deal: they said they'd be convinced I wasn't a car thief if she'd come down to the Hall and pay her two hundred dollars' worth of traffic warrants.

She told me to sit tight while she took a taxi to HYENA headquarters and borrowed money from the bail fund. I asked her if she'd look around for my purse and bring it along.

"I found it awhile ago," she said, "and I realized you'd be locked out. So I sent Kandi to take it to you."

"Did she phone when I didn't turn up?"

"Why, no. I guess she's still waiting for you."

"Rebecca, my dear, Elena said you looked stunning, but my God!" Jeannette von Phister, the founder of HYENA, pecked my cheek, and I turned to introduce Parker, but he wasn't there. I figured he'd wandered off.

"Twenty-five dollars at Magnarama," I said. "The whole outfit."

Jeannette herself, in a decorous brown wool dress, looked, as always, like a well-groomed publicist. Though she called herself a "retired call girl," there was a malicious rumor that she'd never turned a trick in her life.

"I just got here," she said. "Elena asked me because I set it up—I wouldn't say that's procuring, under the circumstances, would you? Isn't it a kick?"

"Especially for the likes of me," I said.

32

Jeannette raised an eyebrow. "Come, now. You make a great-looking little hooker. Are we still having dinner tomorrow night?"

"Of course."

"Seven-thirty," she said, "at the Washington Square Bar and Grill. I've got a proposition for you."

And she was off before I could make any witless jokes about propositions.

I looked around for Parker, but I didn't see him, and I didn't like the way a big blond guy was watching me, so I sat back down and started playing.

I tend to forget everything else when I'm playing, so I was in a sort of trance for about the next forty-five minutes, but it wasn't so deep that I didn't observe two things: The FDOs knew how to have a good time, and my clients were perfect ladies.

Some of the guests were excellent dancers and a good many of them had hollow legs, if the number of empty glasses was any indication.

As for the hostesses, they were equally gracious to guests of both sexes, and they did not behave in a bawdy or provocative way—which is more than I can say for a good number of the guests. Of both sexes.

When I stopped playing again, I made another stab at trying to find Parker. I didn't find him, but for some reason it didn't bother me. I don't think it even entered my head that he'd leave the party without telling me why. I just assumed we were somehow missing each other.

There was champagne at the bar, and I poured myself some. "Cheers," said a male voice, and a glass clinked against mine. "You been in this business long?"

The voice belonged to a tall, broad man, probably in his late thirties but not very well preserved, the same man I'd seen watching me earlier. He had sandy hair and a face that missed being handsome because it was overly florid and a little on the mean side.

I saw no reason to go all fluttery and say I knew he wouldn't believe it, but actually I was a Montgomery Street lawyer helping out a friend. So I lied. "Not very," I said.

"I thought not. How'd you happen to get into this line of work?"

I told Elena's story about the woman professor who'd taught her everything she knew.

The man laughed and offered his hand. "My name's Frank. What's yours?"

"Rebecca."

"May I call you Becky?"

"AbsoLUTEly not. Never. Not if you paid me a thousand dollars."

He leaned over and whispered, "How much would it take?"

"To get me to—oh. You mean to . . ."

He nodded.

I laughed, trying to recover my equilibrium. "The going rate's a hundred dollars," I said, as if I were used to saying it. "But this isn't that kind of party."

"What do you mean?"

"I mean it's just a party. Music, dancing, champagne. That's it. Didn't you bring a date?"

"No."

"Too bad. Some other time then." I picked up my glass and sauntered back to the piano, perhaps swinging my hips the least bit more than strictly necessary.

It was getting late, and I thought something moderately quiet might be nice. I played "Sentimental Journey," then "Cry Me a River." But somehow a romantic mood didn't fall like a mantle over the party, so I gave in and tried some livelier tunes. It was the right thing to do; those FDOs were in a mood to boogie.

Since Elena had told me the place was soundproofed, I packed up my inhibitions and played "Rock Around the Clock." That was such a hit, I let loose with a spate of oldies-but-goodies that had every foot in the house tapping and most of them dancing. I was giving them a rest with "Blueberry

Hill,'' when I saw Parker come in the door. He looked strained and a bit unsteady. I was afraid he was ill.

The foyer was crowded with dancing couples, among them a rotund FDO and Kandi, entwined drunken-sailor-style. Kandi had her head on the fat chap's shoulder, and her eyes may have been closed. I don't know if she saw Parker or not.

Parker sunk a hand into the folds of Fatty's neck and came up with Kandi's wrist. She looked up, and he said something to her, but I couldn't hear what it was. I heard her, though. She said, ''Parker. What are you doing here?'' She disentangled herself from Fatty as if he were a stuffed animal she was bored with, and led Parker out of my line of vision.

I heard both their voices, angry and getting angrier. I couldn't distinguish the words, but I imagined the dancers could, so I stopped in the middle of ''Blueberry Hill'' and again swung into ''Rock Around the Clock,'' which is the loudest song I know.

And that's when those fun-loving FDOs staged their adorable phony raid. You know what happened after that—I rescued one of California's most prestigious perverts and wound up in the slammer.

CHAPTER 7

Elena turned up to get me out just before 2:00 A.M., proved she was actually Elena Mooney, Mustang owner, paid the $200, and I was a free woman.

She'd kept her taxi waiting, so I was home in about seven minutes. A red Volkswagen was parked in my space, and Elena said it was Kandi's. No one was inside it.

"She must have gone inside," said Elena. "It's been about an hour and a half since I sent her. Call me in the morning, and I'll come get you and drive you back to get your car. It's the least I can do."

I gave her the keys to the Mustang and told her where to find it.

Stuck halfway into my mailbox slot, so that it could be easily extracted, was a folded piece of lined paper from a pocket notebook. I unfolded it and read: "R—US w/p. K." I took it to mean "upstairs with purse" and mentally applauded Kandi for being so cryptic. This is always wise, I think, when leaving notes practically in public. The only thing was, if I hadn't talked to Elena first, I wouldn't have known who "K" was. But this was a quibble: she'd have identified herself through the intercom as soon as I rang the doorbell. I pressed the button to prove it.

No one answered, so I figured she was asleep. Since there's a little overhang in the entryway where the mailboxes are, I wasn't getting wet, but it was two-thirty and I wanted to go to bed. I rang a lot more times—more than I needed to, because I was getting damned impatient. But still nobody answered.

There was nothing to do but ring the other doorbells until someone answered. I'd probably wake someone up, but it couldn't be helped. I pressed the manager's bell first, because it's her job to be inconvenienced.

Her voice was husky over the intercom: "What is it?"

"Mrs. Garcia, it's Rebecca Schwartz. I'm locked out. Could you buzz me in?"

"Oh Lord. Okay, come to my apartment for your key. I'm too tired to meet you at yours."

"It's okay. I have an extra key on the doorsill. All you have to do is buzz me through the gate."

She did, and I said thanks, but she didn't answer.

I'm foolhardy enough to keep a key on my doorsill because I have a tendency to lock myself out when I go to the garbage chute. It's not the safest thing in the world, but I feel like an idiot having to beg Mrs. Garcia to let me in my own apartment, so I'm willing to take the chance.

I decided I'd probably wake up everybody in the building except Kandi if I banged on the door. I'd use the extra key and if I scared her, it was too bad. I felt for it and unlocked the door. Even though the lights were on, I reached automatically for the light switch to the right of the door. I did it even though I could plainly see that someone had ransacked my house and left Kandi dead on my Flokati rug. The mind is a funny thing.

Kandi was lying half-on and half-off the rug, with one leg kind of folded under her and the other stretched out under the aquarium stand. Her hair and my rug were stained and so was the base of my Don Quixote statue, which had been tossed carelessly on the rug, apparently after serving to bash Kandi's brains out. (I meant that figuratively—there weren't any brains in view. If there had been, I know for a fact I'd have screamed, which I didn't.) I suppose Kandi must have fought for her life because a lot of fluffy apricot feathers had settled on the rug and on my two white sofas. I think I hated the feathers most of all. They reminded me of something: a cat Gary and I had kept that came and went as it pleased through a cat door. More than once, we came home and found feathers all over the living room. That was the cat's way of showing us he'd made a kill. I hadn't had much experience with death, but I associated feathers with it.

A few books had been torn from my bookcase, my purse and Kandi's had been emptied on the coffee table, and the sofa pillows were on the floor. That was about all there was to the ransacking. As you already know, there aren't many secret crannies in my living room.

Now, as I have mentioned, I did not scream. But I wasn't altogether brave and true about the situation either. I probably should have gone and felt Kandi's pulse to make sure she was dead. But I didn't; I just assumed she was.

After absorbing death and ransacking, my quicksilver brain hopped right on to the next subject: the whereabouts of the murderer. He might still be in the apartment, and it wasn't big enough for both of us.

I stepped out in the hall and locked the door. This was silly, because you don't need a key to unlock it from the inside, and Kandi had brought one with her. But I did it anyway. Remember, I'd reached for the switch even though the lights were on. I wasn't thinking too clearly.

Although it's Mrs. Garcia's job to be inconvenienced, I didn't go to her apartment. I went to Tony Larson's. I did this not because he is a man and she is a woman, but because he lives next door. I figured no murderer would have the *chutzpah* to sashay out my door with me banging and hollering right outside. If he was there, I'd have him trapped.

I banged and hollered. Tony came to the door still wrapping some sort of Japanese robe around him that came to about mid-thigh. I had thought he might still be up, since he's a bartender and the bars don't close until two. As it turned out, he was and so was his date; they just didn't have any clothes on.

Apparently, Tony grasped the urgency of the situation,

because he didn't complain that I'd halted Cupid on his appointed rounds and he didn't comment on my outfit. He put his arms around me and I let him. Just for a second. Then I got down to business:

"There's a dead woman in my apartment."

"Christ," said Tony and started out the door, but I caught him.

"Wait, Tony. She's been murdered. I don't know if anyone's in there or not. Have you got a gun?"

"Yeah. Wait here."

He went to his hall closet and came back with a hunting rifle. I unlocked my door and we went in, tiptoeing. But we might as well have marched in combat boots, because Tony lost his cool when he saw Kandi.

"Christ," he said again.

"There's only four places to hide," I said. "The kitchen, the bedroom closet, the hall closet, and the bathroom. Go over near the piano so you can cover me and the door to the hall while I look in the kitchen."

He did, and I stepped gingerly to the kitchen counter and peeped over it. There was no one there. I let him do the rest of the place alone, so I'd be free to sound the alarm if he got into any trouble. He didn't.

"There's no one here," he reported. "But the rest of the place is pretty well ransacked too. And there's a pair of rubber kitchen gloves lying on your bed. Come to my house and we'll call the cops."

At Tony's, a pretty young woman, by now decently clad in jeans and a sweater, was pouring brandy into three snifters. "I could hear you from the bedroom," she said. "Is everything okay?"

"No," I said, reaching gratefully for a snifter, "but at least no one's there."

"Rebecca, this is Marilyn. She'll show you where the phone is," said Tony, and he left to put on some clothes.

Sitting down in a beanbag chair, I let Marilyn bring me the phone, which was on a long cord. My mother would have

been proud of the way I handled it. I dialed "O" and asked
for the number of the San Francisco police, and then I dialed
the number. "I'd like to report a murder, please," I said, as
calm as if I were ordering something from Saks.

The police officer gave me something called "communications," and I repeated my request.

They asked me for my name, phone number, and address.
I told them I was next door and gave them Tony's number
and address, which was a good thing because they called
right back to make sure I wasn't a crank.

When that was done, I asked Tony if I could use the bathroom and Marilyn if she had a hairbrush I could borrow.
They both said yes.

Alone, I took off Elena's turban and my make-up and
brushed my hair into its accustomed professional do.

"That's better," Tony said. "You looked like a ten-dollar
hooker. Where have you been, anyway?"

"Playing the piano in a whorehouse."

"Okay, be snotty."

"Honest. The dead woman worked there."

"No kidding? She's a hooker?"

"No and yes."

"Who killed her?"

"I don't know. I got no idea how I'm going to explain any
of this to the cops, much less to my mom. Or where I'm
going to sleep tonight." I shivered. "Not over there."

"I could give you the key to my apartment," said Marilyn.
"I'm going to stay with Tony."

"No thanks. I think I need company. I'd better call my
sister."

I dialed Mickey's number in Berkeley. Her nogoodnik
boyfriend answered, "Whaddaya want?" But he wasn't being rude because it was 3:00 A.M. He always answers like
that, the way some people say, "Kelly's Brickyard."

I said, "Mickey. Now."

"She ain't here."

"Alan, I am in no mood for jokes. Now." He put her on.

"You tell El Creepo," I said, "that when someone calls at three A.M., it is undoubtedly an emergency and no time to play games."

"What emergency?"

"A lady of doubtful virtue is dead on my Flokati rug, and I would like you to get your shapely tush across the Bay Bridge fifteen minutes ago."

"Shall I bring a vat of acid to dispose of the body?"

"Mickey, I'm serious."

"Christ. One of your clients?"

"Yes." This wasn't strictly true, but it was close enough.

"Do Mom and Dad know?"

Tony's buzzer went off. "Mickey, the cops just got here. Will you get on the stick? And leave Kruzick where he is."

Since she hung up without saying good-bye, I guess she got the idea I wanted her to hurry.

The cops were not homicide inspectors but uniformed officers from a radio car, come to make a "preliminary investigation." It seems the police never take your word for anything. They looked at Kandi without touching her—so maybe I really didn't do wrong by failing to take her pulse—and called an ambulance. One of them stayed with the body, and the other one took me back to Tony's.

"Look," I asked him, "how long is this going to take?" I was worried about imposing on Tony and Marilyn.

"Can't say. An hour or two, probably. Maybe more."

"Can I go back to my apartment, then?"

"Afraid not."

Tony and Marilyn looked at each other. "We could go to your house," Tony said to her, but his heart wasn't in it.

Marilyn shook her head. "Let's stay with Rebecca, at least till Mickey gets here." It was nice of them to stay with me, but I think there was an element besides altruism in their decision: They didn't want to miss anything, and I can't say I blamed them. It's pretty awful to find a corpse in your apartment, but you can't help being curious if it's safely next door.

Pretty soon the ambulance came, and I went back home

to see what the steward did. He listened for a heart and pulse beat and told the officers to call the coroner and homicide department. Kandi was now officially dead.

At the time, I didn't understand why they just didn't send homicide inspectors in the beginning, but I've since learned it was because they were "on call" at home asleep. So the officers called "communications," which phoned the inspectors on call, and presumably the photo lab and crime lab as well, because their myrmidons arrived about the same time as Inspectors Phil Martinez and Leo Curry, who were wearing brown suits and looking like you would if somebody woke you up in the middle of the night and said come to work.

They all went into my apartment, leaving one of the cops from the radio car with me and sending the other out to question the neighbors. He started with Tony and Marilyn, who hadn't seen or heard anything.

My sister Mickey arrived just after the coroner's wagon. In fact, my apartment door was open for the fellows from that office when Mickey walked by on her way to Tony's, and I was sorry she had to see what it looked like in there. Especially when she collapsed in my arms.

Mickey is twenty-four and a graduate student in psychology. Her name is actually Michaela, but "Mickey" fits her better for now. In a few years, she'll grow into three syllables.

She is the "pretty one" in the family—more slender and darker than I am, with long, wavy brown hair. Her taste in men runs to unemployed actors, but otherwise she is a good kid.

Tony and Marilyn gave her some brandy, but I couldn't have any, on orders of the San Francisco Police Department. Cops feel more secure with sober witnesses.

Right after Mickey got there, the cops sent for me. There was fingerprint powder everywhere. "Which of this property is yours?" asked Martinez.

"Everything except that purse and its contents," I told

him, pointing to Kandi's things. He let me go back. By now it was well after three o'clock, and Tony and Marilyn had had enough. They went to Marilyn's, leaving me Tony's extra key to lock up with.

Then came the catechism.

Martinez left Curry hovering about the body and made himself comfortable with Mickey and me. I was faced with a dilemma. I didn't want to tell him Elena ran a bordello, or that Kandi worked there, but I'd have to say where I'd been. If I told them Elena's address, they might go there to question her—and one look at the place, along with Elena's rap sheet, would give her game away. This was not my problem, of course, and as an officer of the court, I was supposed to be against law-breaking, which Elena was engaged in, but she was a friend. Even if she had sent me out in the rain with Senator Cuckoo and caused me to spend two hours in the bucket.

I decided to give the street, but say I'd forgotten the number.

I reeled off the whole *megillah*, leaving out the address, the "raid," and the senator's name. I stuck to my earlier story about leaving the party to take a sick friend to the hospital. Only the way I told it this time, I made the friend just a party guest whose name I didn't know, saying I was doing Elena a favor. That much was true, anyway. Martinez came right out and asked if the "sick" person were having a drug reaction. I said I didn't know, but that was my guess.

"Okay," said Martinez. "Do you know what time the victim left the party?"

"You'll have to ask Elena. I was a guest of the San Francisco Police at the time."

"How did you know Kandi was inside the apartment?"

"Elena said she would be. Besides, she'd left me a note in the mailbox."

"May I see it?"

I'd forgotten all about it, and it took me a minute to remember where I'd put it. Since I hadn't had my purse, there was only one choice. Mildly embarrassed, I fished it out of my bosom.

"Is this some kind of code?" asked Martinez.

"I don't think so. I assumed it meant 'upstairs with purse.'"

"Is it possible the P is a person's initial?"

"Not so far as I know. Especially since it's lower case."

"But the 'u' and the 's' are upper case."

"Yes. I thought that was meant to show it wasn't the word 'us.' She could have used small letters with periods after them, but that would have been more confusing because they were part of the same word instead of two separate words."

I'll never understand how women's minds work."

I flared. "I don't have to take that kind of stuff. I'm trying to be as helpful as I can, even though I flinch every time someone else puts black powder on my nice walls, and even though I found the body of a woman I hardly know on my living room floor, and even though my house is full of strangers and . . ."

"Okay, okay." He held up a hand. It was a good thing he stopped me because I was about to cast doubt on his intelligence and possibly his ancestry, which might have been going too far.

"I'm sorry about the fingerprint powder," he said, picking the least of the problems, like the classic lady with a broken leg wailing about a run in her nylons. "But I'm afraid we'll have to do the whole apartment, since it's been ransacked. Who do you think did that?"

I must have looked at him like he'd gone *meshugge*. "The murderer, I suppose."

"Not Kandi?"

"I don't see why she would have. If she wanted to rob me, she'd have just gone through my bureau for money and jewelry. But since she'd announced herself with a note in my mailbox, it wouldn't have been very smart."

"So why should the murderer? If he was a burglar that Kandi surprised, why wouldn't he just go through your bureau? Why look under the sofa pillows and behind the books in the bookcase?''

''I don't know.'' I thought about it. ''Maybe he knew Kandi. Maybe he thought she'd hidden something here.''

''Any idea what it might have been?''

''No.''

''How do you suppose he got in?''

''Either he broke in before Kandi got here, or she let him in.''

''Or they arrived together and his initial was 'P.' Think. Did you and Kandi have any mutual acquaintances with that initial?''

''So far as I know, Elena was our only mutual acquaintance.''

Inspector Curry came back in. ''Anything?'' asked Martinez.

''Yeah. Nobody saw anybody who didn't belong here except a couple on the third floor who got in about 1:45. A fellow walked up as they were unlocking the downstairs gate and said he was on his way to see Miss Schwartz. So they let him in. No one saw the deceased enter the building, and no one heard anything.''

''Miss Schwartz's caller—what'd he look like?''

''Tall, brown hair, tweed jacket, yellow turtleneck.''

''Miss Schwartz?''

''Parker!'' I blurted.

''P as in Parker. Now that's very interesting, Miss Schwartz. Who might Parker be?''

''He was my date for the party. We got separated. I suppose he came by to make sure I got home all right.''

''What's his last name?''

''Phillips.''

''Now that's even more interesting. Considering that was the victim's last name. Did you look at her driver's license?''

''No.''

''I did. Her full name was Carol Phillips.''

Things I hadn't put together came back to me in a rush.

Parker had a sister, Carol, who was a student at San Francisco State. Parker had left the party without a word to me and then come back and talked to Kandi angrily. Was Kandi that Carol Phillips? Could the elegant Parker have a prostitute for a sister?

I suppose I must have reacted somehow, because Martinez said, "That name mean anything to you?"

"Parker has a sister named that. But I've never seen her. I don't know if Kandi was she."

"How well do you know Parker?"

"I've known him about three weeks. I met him at my law partner's house."

"I said how well."

"None of your business."

"Okay, Miss Schwartz. I guess that's enough for now. What's his address and phone number?"

"You're crazy."

Martinez picked up my phone and dialed directory assistance. He asked for Elena's number as well as Parker's, but she wasn't listed. Martinez asked me for her number.

"I've forgotten it."

"Well, you've got till tomorrow to remember. We'll keep in touch."

Everybody had cleared out now except Martinez and Curry. "Are you through in my apartment?" I asked.

"For tonight," said Martinez. "But we'll have to seal it overnight and have the lab people go over it inch by inch in the morning. Are you planning to stay with your sister?"

"Yes."

"You'd better give me the phone number. I may need you."

I gave it to him. "When can I come home tomorrow?"

"Probably around ten o'clock. Eleven to be safe. I'd like to ask you to do one last thing before you go, though. Will you come over and take a look to see if anything's missing?"

"Okay." Martinez showed me around my own apartment

and I took a cursory look, which was the best I could do without touching anything.

When we got to the bedroom, he pointed to the rubber gloves on the bed. "Those yours?"

"They look like mine. I keep them under the sink."

We looked there; my gloves were gone. "He must have worn them to avoid leaving fingerprints."

Martinez didn't answer.

"Nothing's missing that I can see," I said. "But did your fellows find anything that—well—that looked like it didn't belong here?"

"You mean the mythical object the murderer was looking for? No, Miss Schwartz, they didn't. Sometimes, you know, a murderer will ransack a place as a cover-up—to make it look like an interrupted burglary."

I went back to Tony's while Martinez and Curry locked up. Mickey, who had sat there like a scared statue while those apes were there, came to life with a shudder. "Let's get out of here," she said.

"Not quite yet. I have to think a minute."

I thought: I could call Parker and warn him, but what good would that do? If Kandi had been his sister, I'd have to break the news that she was dead. An unpleasant prospect. Or if he'd killed her, I'd be tipping him off, and that would be obstructing justice. I put the thought out of my mind. We didn't know each other very well, but I was sure he wouldn't kill his own sister. At least I told myself I was. I decided not to call.

I could call Mom and Dad, but that would just frighten them. The murder had been discovered too late to make the morning papers, so I had plenty of time to let them know before the mass media did.

There was only one call I couldn't avoid making. I had lied to the police on Elena's account, which put me in the position of having to make sure our stories jibed. Besides, if I had her call the police instead of just letting them come around, it might save her the embarrassment of having them pay a call at an awkward moment.

I dialed and explained the situation. "Jesus!" she said. "Kandi was a rotten little bitch, but who'd want to murder—"

"Listen, Elena, you're in a spot. You're going to have to talk to the police. If you call them first thing in the morning, maybe you can avoid having them drop in."

"I see what you mean. Omigod. This probably means I'm going to have to close down."

"It's about time you went straight anyhow. Look, I recognized Senator Handley, but I didn't tell the cops who he was. I gave them some story about a sick friend, but the truth is going to have to come out, I'm afraid. Kandi knew the senator, and I suppose he might have killed her for some reason. Get in touch with him and tell him to tell the cops he was at the party."

"Oh, Rebecca, I can't—"

"You've got to. If he doesn't tell them, I will."

"I see. Okay, I'll talk to him." She sighed and said goodbye.

Mickey and I turned off the lights, locked Tony's place, and left. The minute we were in her car, the tears started coming. I do okay for a Marin County Jewish princess, but Superwoman I'm not.

CHAPTER
8

I blubbered out the story to Mickey, leaving out only the senator's identity. She was a good listener. A good sister, too. She said anybody would have wanted to go to Elena's party, and no one could have foreseen it was going to get me involved in a traffic accident and a murder. She also said I acquitted myself handsomely with the cops and she wished she had as much presence of mind. Okay, so I'm bragging, but remember, I also told you I cried.

Mickey even tried to get my mind off Parker by dragging red herrings across the path. She said maybe Elena killed Kandi.

"After all," she argued, "Elena was the only one we know of who actually knew where Kandi was. She could have followed her there and done her in."

"But she was home when I called from the Hall," I reminded her.

"Okay. Perfect. She could have gone to your place before she went to HYENA headquarters, beaned Kandi, and torn up the place in about ten minutes. Maybe Kandi'd robbed her and she was trying to get the money back. In fact, maybe the $200 she gave the cops came out of the . . ."

"Oh, stop. She came in a taxi. The driver'd know she stopped there."

Mickey waved a dismissing hand. "Details."

She stopped the car in front of the old stucco house where she and Alan shared the first-floor flat. It was furnished

Berkeley-style, with bricks and boards for bookcases, cast-off furniture picked up at garage sales, and a stereo that was probably worth as much as the rest of the furniture put together.

We made up a bed for me on the Goodwill couch, and I got out of my bedraggled finery. I'd forgotten to pack anything, so I used Mickey's toothbrush, borrowed a T-shirt for pajamas, and turned in. I was nearly asleep when I heard the thud of the morning paper on the porch.

The next thing I knew, somebody was shaking me awake. From the light, it was pretty early morning. "Phone," said Mickey. "It's Parker. The cops told him where to find you."

I tumbled out of bed, quick. "Parker. Are you all right?"

"I'm in jail. Booked for suspicion of murdering my own sister." He sounded miserable.

"Oh God, Parker. I'm so sorry."

"Thanks. I need a lawyer."

"You'd better tell me what happened."

"It all happened so fast I hardly know. These guys Martinez and Curry showed up and told me about Carol and asked if she was my sister. Then, before I could even assimilate that, they asked me about my movements last night. I *had* been to your house—I don't know if you know that."

"I gathered. Was your sister there at the time?"

"I don't know. No one answered the door, so I went away. Anyway, the cops asked me if I'd take a polygraph test, and I said no. I was nervous, and I didn't see any point in it. My God, my sister was dead!

"So then they sent a lab guy to get my fingerprints, and they stayed with me while he went back to the Hall of Justice. After a while, he called and told Martinez something, and Martinez asked me if I'd ever touched that funny statue you have on the coffee table."

"I suppose you know that was the murder weapon."

"I do now, anyway. I said I couldn't remember touching it."

"But, Parker, you must have. Sometime in my apartment."

"I just can't remember it. But I must have, because they found one of my prints on it. They told me that, and I still couldn't remember, and the next thing I knew they advised me of my rights and brought me down here."

The more miserable he sounded, the stronger I felt, and I didn't like it. Florence Nightingale Schwartz was back in business.

"Okay, Parker, two things. First, tell them you'll take the polygraph."

"No!"

"Why not?"

"I don't believe in it. I don't like it. It's an invasion of privacy."

"But they're holding you for murder."

"Can't you get me out on bail?"

"That's the other thing. I'm horribly afraid you're going to have to spend the weekend in jail; they can hold you without charging you till Monday, and if they do charge you, they don't have to arraign you till Tuesday. I'm not at all sure I can get you out before then."

"But you'll try?"

"Of course. I'll have to call a judge at home. I'll do that, and then I'll come over to City Prison as soon as I can. Try to take it easy, okay?"

"Thanks, Rebecca."

It was seven o'clock—I'd never get Parker bailed out if I called a judge at that hour. Mickey had gone back to bed, and I had no alarm to set, so I just lay down again, hoping I'd wake up about nine.

I did, mostly because Alan was playing the stereo in the bedroom.

Since I had no idea what judge was on call for the weekend, I called the cops and flung myself on the mercy of the desk sergeant. Luckily, I got a nice one; he said it was Judge Rinaldo.

I extolled Parker's virtues at some length for Rinaldo's benefit, but he said he'd have to call homicide and get back to me.

Depressed, I knocked on the bedroom door to beg for one of Mickey's robes. Mickey had gone out for a minute, so Alan made the loan. Then he hovered while I made coffee. Instead of helping with the coffee, he offered conversation that made my teeth itch:

"What's it like to find a stiff in your living room?"

"She was a human being, Alan."

"Now she's a piece of meat."

"Haven't you got any compassion?"

"Not for some doxie I never met. I'm saving it all for my poor, traumatized, old-maid sister-in-law. Must have been kind of tough on you, huh?"

Alan's all right, really. It's just that he has trouble remembering he's not on stage all the time. If you don't watch him, he does bits, like the tough-guy routine he was affecting this morning. Also, he has no sense of responsibility and will probably never make a decent living. But he's got a good heart, deep down. That and a lot of curly hair.

I said it wasn't exactly uplifting, finding Kandi, but I wasn't his sister-in-law.

"Did your new boyfriend do it?"

"How do I know?"

"Well, I hope not. I was kind of hoping you'd marry him. Then your sister wouldn't have to worry about you anymore."

"Worry about me? She's living in sin with Mr. Putz and she should worry about *me*?"

"You'll get used to me in thirty or forty years."

"I'll brain you first," I said, and instantly wished I hadn't. It brought back a mental picture I could do without.

Alan picked up a cast-iron casserole and held it out. "Here.

No time like the present. Come on, get it over with. Face it, Rebecca, you've been wanting to for two years.''

He stretched out his arms, practically begging for it, and looked at the ceiling. " 'Ay, but to die and go we know not where,' " he said, " 'To lie in cold obstruction and to rot . . .' "

I took the casserole and lifted it in what I hoped was a threatening gesture, but I doubt he even noticed, he was so full of himself: " 'This sensible warm motion to become a kneaded clod; and the delighted spirit . . .' "

If that had gone on much longer, I probably *would* have killed him, but Mickey saved his life by making a grand entrance with a fragrant paper bag. He shut up, and I lowered the casserole. "I was about to do you a favor," I said to Mickey.

Alan sneaked up behind her and nuzzled her ear: "Would you have missed this sensible warm motion, hmmm?"

She shook him off. "You children behave. I've brought breakfast." She opened the bag and started arranging croissants on a plate. The pastries were a real extravagance on the kind of budget she and Jerko lived on. It disoriented Alan so much he set the table.

I poured coffee and orange juice, and Mickey dredged up some butter and strawberry preserves. After three croissants and two cups of coffee, I felt a lot better. Strong enough to talk to Mom and Dad. I would have called them, too, if Mom hadn't beat me to the punch. The phone rang just about then.

"Hi, Mom," said Mickey. "Oh, she's with us. Certainly she's all right. I'll prove it."

She passed me the receiver. "Thank God you're all right, darling," said Mom. "I called and you weren't home."

"I know, Mom. I'm not at home a lot. I can drive and everything. But just this once, there *is* a little something wrong. I was going to call you before you heard it on the radio, but . . ."

"The radio? What, has your house burned down?"

"No, Mom. Now listen. Someone was killed there."

"What, in your building? I knew it wasn't safe on Telegraph Hill. Just last year they killed a girl in her own bed."

"Her husband killed her. Look, the killing was in my
apartment."

"*Your* apartment? Oy. Are you sure you're all right, darling? I could come right over."

"I'm okay. I wasn't there at the time. I'd left my purse at
a party. She—the victim—came to return it, and she got there
before I did. By the time I got home, she was dead. Somconc
bashed her with my Don Quixote sculpture."

"Thank God it wasn't you!"

"The police don't seem to think it was a burglary. My
house was ransacked, but nothing was missing."

"So why ransack it?"

"To make it look like a burglary, I guess. Or maybe because the murderer thought Kandi—the dead woman—had
brought something that he wanted."

"*Bubpkes!*"

"Can I talk to Daddy? I'd like to tell him, too."

"He had to run an errand. I'll tell him. Listen, should we
call off the party?" My parents' thirtieth wedding anniversary party was scheduled for the next day. Sunday.

"What, are you crazy?" I said. "*I'm* not dead."

"But, darling, you're upset. Party or no party, my children
come first."

"Mom, I'll have a great time. Everyone'll want to talk to
me because I'll be notorious."

"You sure? It's not too late."

"Positive. Listen, I've got to go home and put my house
back together."

"You're not going back to the place alone?"

"Mickey will drive me. I'll have her come in and make
sure no one's there."

"You're not under suspicion, are you, dear?"

"No, Mom. They've arrested a friend of mine. I'm his
lawyer." Once that was out, I had to tell her the whole story,

and I believe she was more upset by my going to a party at a bordello than she was about the murder.

Not being able to fit into any of Mickey's jeans, I had to wear my silver blouse and black skirt back to my house. I looked as grubby as I felt. I contemplated a shower and then a blitz of my house, but I knew the blitz would have to wait until I'd seen Parker.

Mickey didn't want to go in with me, because it meant taking me to my car, then driving all the way back to Telegraph Hill. But I needed her to help me move furniture. That Flokati rug had cost me $150 on sale at Macy's and I wasn't about to throw it out; I planned to wash the bloodstains out in the bathtub.

We found the place in worse disarray than the night before, if that was possible. But I didn't let myself think about it. Mickey and I heaved the sofas and coffee table off the rug, and I gathered it up while she ran some cold water. Then she left me alone.

I added detergent and left the rug to soak while I called Judge Rinaldo. "I'm sorry, Miss Schwartz," he said. "Martinez and Curry are dead against bail for your client. They've got witnesses and fingerprints."

"Yes, but he's not a flight risk."

"They say he's in such a depressed state he might try suicide."

"Bull—" I stopped myself just in time. "I mean, nonsense! I talked to him this morning."

"I'm sorry," the judge repeated. "You'll have a bail hearing if he's charged." He hung up.

It was no more than I expected. The bit about suicide disturbed me, though. I hadn't thought Parker was that upset, but then he had rather unreasonably refused to take the polygraph test. Unreasonably if he were innocent, that is. I had to assume he was innocent, so why not take the test? Was he really so upset he just wasn't thinking straight? Could be; I would be if I were in his shoes. But so upset he was suicidal?

I hoped to God not. And not only on his account—I wanted a man I didn't have to mother.

I went back to the rug. A little scrubbing and the blood came out pretty easily, but the feathers were something else again. Even after I'd gotten bored picking them off, you could hardly see the difference. So I decided to vacuum it when it was dry, and addressed myself to the hard part of the task: wringing the damn thing out.

Then I bathed, put on a white silk shirt, gray flannel slacks, and a coral necklace. That was good enough for a Saturday at the Hall of Justice.

CHAPTER 9

The Hall of Justice was eerily quiet. I took the elevator to City Prison and asked to see my client. The cops showed us into an interview room about the size of my bathroom, painted in two shades of blue. Two ugly shades. It was furnished with a table and two chairs.

As soon as they left us alone, we kissed and held each other for a long time. Parker's eyes were red, from either crying or lack of sleep. Maybe both.

"No bail?" he asked, sitting down.

I shook my head. "I'm sorry. Martinez and Curry told the judge you might be suicidal."

"Christ, I just might be." He waved his hand in a futile gesture. I put a notebook and pen in the middle of the table so he'd have something to fidget with. "I'm having a very hard time believing any of this is actually happening."

"I know. So am I. But we've got to talk about it."

"Yes. Rebecca, she was only twenty-four. God! Just twenty-four!" He picked up the pen and made two fists around it. "I remember how jealous I was when she was born. Everyone adored her because she was so pretty. I did too, by the time I got over my jealousy.

"It's funny the things you remember." Animation came into his voice. "Mom had a black velvet cape that she used to wear to the opera.

"One day—around Halloween—I got a pair of those fake glasses with a nose and mustache. You know, Groucho Marx glasses—and I put them on along with the velvet cape and sneaked up behind Carol. We used to watch that weekly horror show on TV—*Creature Feature*, I think they call it now—and we'd recently seen one of the versions of 'Dracula.' Anyway, I tapped her on the shoulder and she screamed. No one else was home, so I could do anything I wanted. I chased her around the house for about ten minutes, until finally I cornered her and she just kind of sunk down, whimpering.

"She was so defenseless and so terrified and so *pretty*, I realized I loved her.

"I was a teenager, and she was only about seven; I wasn't used to moments of sentiment. I picked her up and took off the glasses. She put her arms around my neck and wouldn't let go."

Parker's voice was choked, but he went on. "She was, well, wild in high school. Ran away from home, and we didn't hear from her for over a year. She came home strung out. She got straight and stayed home long enough to graduate. Then she went away again. To San Francisco. This time she kept in touch, and in a way that was even more heartbreaking. We knew she was on every kind of drug but heroin. Acid, speed, downers—coke, I guess, when she could get it. She'd always been a bright girl, and she was wasting herself. She was a vegetable. I swear to God, all she said was 'Hey, man' and 'Far out' for three years. But a couple of years ago her boyfriend got busted for dealing, and that seemed to sober her up.

"She wrote me that she was going back to school. Our parents had stopped giving her money a long time ago, so I offered to do what I could. She said no, she had a job as a waitress. And I respected her for that. For not taking money. If I'd known what she was doing . . ."

He put a hand over his eyes. I patted it and told him to take a break while I got him some water.

Perhaps I should tell you now that I wasn't exactly pleased by this narrative. Here I was, looking for a man I wouldn't have to mother, and I had a six-footer crying all over me. I told myself I was being unreasonable; that people go through periods of unhappiness and have to help each other through them; that Parker would do the same for me if the roles were reversed. But our relationship was just beginning, and this was no way to start. In retrospect, it seems funny that I thought that, when I didn't even know if he was about to confess to murder or what, but I did. I'm afraid it wasn't a very professional attitude.

If what I said seems cold, let me tell you that I was nearly in tears myself. That was the trouble.

I got the water, and he drank it. "Anyway," he began again, "when I saw her at Elena's, you can imagine how I felt. I saw her right after you'd told me you could tell the hookers by the length of their skirts. I saw a pair of legs and I looked at them first, and then there was . . . was Carol. I couldn't take it in. I mean I did and I didn't. Do you know what I mean?"

"Yes," I said. "That's what happens when you get a shock. You know it's true because your senses tell you, but you resist it. Because you want it not to be true."

He took my hand and squeezed it. "Exactly, yes. Well, I just wanted to get out of there. I didn't want to be in the same room with her. I'm sorry I left you like that, but it was so sudden. . . . It was as if someone else actually walked out of that house. I felt disembodied. I wasn't thinking." I squeezed back to let him know I understood.

"Somehow, I got myself to a bar. I remember getting in the car and not having any idea where to go or what to do, and then I just saw a bar, and I stopped and went in. I didn't even remember where it was."

"What was the name of it?"

"I don't know. Does it matter?"

"Not for now, but maybe later."

"I got drunk. I just sat there drinking one Scotch-and-water after another until I was numb enough to start thinking about it. And then I finally did realize it was true. I was furious. I hadn't felt like that with her before. I mean being a druggie is wasting your life, but this! When she could have done anything she wanted, had all the choices in the world. Drugs are considered—well, a life-style, you know? Some people think they're a way to enlightenment or peace of mind or something; I don't know. It doesn't matter. It's criminal if you're dealing, but it isn't . . . it isn't . . . selling your body.''

"In a way it is."

"No. Not like this."

"I know what you mean. I was just playing devil's advocate. What time did you leave the bar?"

"I'm not sure, really, but I think it must have been around eleven-thirty. I don't know what I had in mind. I guess I thought when she saw me, she'd be so ashamed she'd, you know, give up her life of crime or something. Anyway, I meant to confront her."

"And did you?"

"Well, when I got back there, she was dancing with some fat guy. I grabbed her and called her Carol, and I'm sure, I'm just sure there was a look of shock on her face. But she was a real pro," he said bitterly.

"She wiped it off right away and said, 'What are you doing here?', putting me on the defensive. I said it was obvious what she was doing and that she was coming with me. However I thought she'd react, I was wrong. She wasn't at all contrite. She said, in a pretty snippy way, really, that she was sorry I had to find out, but it was her life and I'd better butt out."

"Is that all?"

"Just about. I couldn't believe she was serious, so I started to harangue her again, but those phony cops came in about then. It's funny. Even after what happened, my only thought was to protect her. I backed her up against a wall so no one could see her, and she let me. The place was bedlam for a while, but then somebody recognized one of the 'cops' and people started laughing. Kind of nervously, you know, getting their bearings, but just glad we weren't all going to jail. Carol must have slipped out from behind me, because the next time I saw her, she was standing with her arm around that fat guy, laughing. As if nothing had happened with me.''

"So what did you do?"

"I wasn't shocked this time; I was just revolted. But I felt the same as before. I just wanted out. So I left. But somehow I still couldn't seem to get it through my head that my sister Carol was really a prostitute. A prostitute, and a nasty little job of work at that. With no family feeling, no affection for me. Perfectly happy to parade herself with guys who weren't fit for her to spit on right in front of her own brother. So I drove to Fort Point, parked, and tried to think. I wasn't in shape for it, though. Remember, I was still pretty drunk. I fell asleep.

"When I woke up, things seemed a lot more real, somehow. The blind rage was gone, and the shock. I understood the position even if I didn't like it. My watch said one-fifteen, and I remembered you for the first time in hours. So I went to your house to apologize.''

"Were you still drunk, Parker? Under normal circumstances, I would have been either still at the party or asleep at that hour.''

"I know. And to answer your question, I was pretty well sobered up. I'm afraid it wasn't the most considerate thing in the world to do. It wasn't only that I wanted to apologize. I needed someone to talk to.''

"What happened when you got there?"

"Some people let me in the front gate, and I went up to your apartment and knocked. Nobody answered, so I figured you were still at Elena's, and I certainly wasn't going back there. I went home and went to bed.''

"When the couple let you in, didn't you notice a note in the mailbox?"

"That note! What the hell is that all about?"

"Did you see it or not?"

"No. The man had his back against the mailboxes, hold-

ing the gate open. I couldn't see them at all. Look here, the
police won't tell me anything. Martinez seems to think I
followed Carol from Elena's and she let me in. Then there's
something about her going downstairs to leave you a note
warning you I was there. Then, according to him, I argued
with her, she refused again to give up her . . . life-style, and
I got violent and killed her. Rebecca, I'm not a violent person. You do believe me, don't you?''

''Of course.''

''Well, tell me what the hell is going on, then. What was
Carol doing in your apartment? And why weren't you there?
And what the devil is this about a note?''

''When those fake cops came in,'' I said, ''Elena figured
she'd need a lawyer. So when the lights went out, she sneaked
me out a back way and told me to drive home, change, and
get ready to make like a lawyer. But I had a minor traffic
accident and spent two hours here at the Hall. Meanwhile,
she found my purse and sent Kandi—I mean Carol—to take
it to my apartment. When the cops finally let me go, I came
home and found the body.''

''What about the note?''

I explained. He whistled. ''So they really think they've got
me.''

''That's not nearly so damaging as the fingerprint. Parker,
you must have touched the statue sometime at my house.''

''I suppose I did, but I honestly can't remember. My God,
I've even considered the idea that I *did* kill her. I don't know—
turned into Mr. Hyde or something.''

''Is that why you won't take the polygraph?''

''You think I'm being silly about that.''

''Yes. Will you reconsider?''

''I'll think about it.''

''I'd better go. Is there anything else I can do? Have the
police notified your parents?''

''They've told them about Carol, yes, but not about me.
They'll be trying to get me. Could you possibly give them a
call?''

"Sure," I said, and took the number. We kissed, and I left, with a promise to come back the next day.

On the way home, I considered the situation. I wasn't lying when I told Parker I believed him, but I was emotionally involved. I *wanted* to believe him. That wouldn't do for a lawyer. If I were going to convince the police or, God forbid, a jury, I'd have to use some sort of evidence besides his lifelong record of good character. Solid citizens are always killing their relatives on a moment's notice.

Martinez's idea about the note was plain crazy. Surely a jury would see that, but I didn't want the case to get that far, and I didn't see any chance of talking Martinez out of his own cockamamie theory.

The fingerprint was damned good evidence for the cops, but of course I didn't know who else's fingerprints were on that sculpture. Mine were, probably. And maybe the real murderer's as well. Or maybe he had worn the rubber gloves. That didn't make sense, though, if it were a crime of passion. More likely he had wiped it.

The base of the sculpture had had blood on it. That meant the murderer must have picked it up by the head to use it as a bludgeon. He might, then, have wiped only the head. If Parker had touched the sculpture somewhere round the middle, his print might have escaped the murderer's ministrations. I'd have to ask Martinez where the print was found.

Something else was bothering me, too. The times didn't seem right. If Parker left the bar at 11:30 to go back to Elena's, he must have gotten there just before 12:00. Midnight would be the traditional time for a practical joke like the raid, so that fit.

I'd called Elena's at a little after 1:00, and she'd already sent Kandi to my apartment. Parker wasn't seen going in until 1:45. Kandi must have been there long before that, and presumably Parker didn't know where she was going. The police theory was that he'd followed her there, so why not go in when she did? There were holes in that, of course; Martinez could argue that he sat in the car getting up his

nerve, or that he and Kandi had talked outside, then she went
in, and Parker followed later. I once heard a D.A. get around
the holes in his theory by saying, "We don't know who made
the unidentified fingerprints; we don't know why the defen-
dant called the police instead of fleeing. We'll probably never
know." And he still got a conviction. Still, the times were a
good place to start. I made a mental note to call Elena.

I let my mind go blank and concentrated on my driving,
but something nagged at me. Something about the idea that
Parker followed Kandi. What was it? I thought for a minute
and it came clear. I didn't know who knew where Kandi was
going. If only Elena did, then *someone* must have followed
her—someone other than Parker. Or, as Mickey suggested,
Elena killed her, having no problem about where to find her.
I needed to find out from Elena who knew where Kandi'd
been sent. Anyway, whether the killer was someone who
knew where Kandi was going or someone who followed her,
he must have been a party guest. That narrowed the field to
about 125 people. Swell.

But if he were someone who followed, how could he tell
which apartment Kandi'd gone into? He wouldn't find her
name on any of the mailboxes. Ah, but he *would* find the
note. Maybe he even watched her scribble and insert it in the
mailbox before she went in.

I remembered I was having dinner with Jeannette von
Phister that night. It would be a good chance to pump her
about Kandi. Parker may not have meant to, but he'd painted
his sister as a rather poisonous little cup of tea. Maybe a lot
of people had reason to kill her.

Then there was the ransacking. As I saw it, there were
three possibilities: Kandi actually had been killed during the
course of a burglary, or the ransacking was done to make it
look like that—the position of the police, no doubt—or the
murderer had been looking for something. Something Kandi
brought there. I decided to proceed on the third hypothesis,
since it looked like the only one that held any hope, from
my point of view. If the killer had been looking for some-

thing, he must have found it, because it wasn't there now. That meant he must still have it. If I could find any evidence at all that such a thing existed, that would strengthen my case a good deal. And if I could find out *who* had it—well!—I might even solve a murder.

I couldn't believe what I saw when I turned into the two-hundred block of Green Street. Two vans bearing the call letters of TV stations were double-parked, and a strange car was in my space. A swarm of humanity buzzed around my building. The dread mass media.

Would they know I was Parker's lawyer? Or care? Probably no to both questions. It must be the address. The police could have told them where Kandi's body had been found and probably who discovered it. They must have come to hear me tell the terrifying tale in my own words. And they'd taken my parking place.

It wasn't reserved, so I couldn't make them move. I drove to the end of the block and turned around. Since it was a Saturday, I figured Telegraph Hill and North Beach would be full of tourists and shoppers, and finding a space would be practically impossible.

These parasites had already caused me considerable inconvenience, and they were about to invade my privacy as well. Briefly, I considered giving them the time-honored slip. I could just go to Chris and Larry's place or somewhere. But then it occurred to me that maybe I could turn the thing to my own advantage. Parker's advantage. The case just might come to trial, and there were plenty of potential jurors out in TV-land. Never too early to start planting the idea that my client was innocent.

It took me fifteen minutes to find a parking place, and then I had to walk back three blocks to my house. But I was glad of the delay. It gave me a chance to plan what I would say. The only thing I was sorry about was wearing a white blouse that day. Anybody knows white isn't good for TV.

I walked up to my gate as if I didn't even notice that twenty-five or thirty people wanted to make me a star.

An unprepossessing sort of fellow with hunched shoulders separated himself from the crush and tugged at my sleeve: "Excuse me, but you wouldn't be Rebecca Schwartz, would you?"

I nodded. He produced a tape recorder and held a microphone in my face. "I'm Dave Schildkraut from radio station KCBS. I was wondering if . . ."

I held up a palm to stop him. "If you don't mind," I said, "I'd like to do it for everyone at once. That way I won't have to repeat myself."

He looked taken aback, but he went back to talk to the others, who were beginning to close in anyway. It seemed I was having a press conference on my front steps. I was shocked at my own chutzpah. Why, I could even go in and change my blouse and no one would blink. But I decided against that. It would look too calculating.

The TV and radio folks arranged themselves in a half moon around me, shoving a thicket of microphones as close as they could. A few poor souls way in the back looked sadly out of date with their pencils and pads: old-timey newspaper reporters.

"Miss Schwartz," said a deep broadcast-voice I vaguely recognized, "could you tell us in your own words what happened last night?"

I told them very concisely that I'd been to a party, had to leave suddenly to run an errand for the hostess—who later found my purse and sent Kandi home with it—and that I'd found the body when I got home.

I left out the part about the accident and being detained at the Hall, because they might like the irony too much: the idea that if I'd been home, maybe Kandi wouldn't have been killed or maybe I would have. Even though it was a Saturday and there wouldn't be much news to compete with the murder, I wanted to make sure I got to say the important stuff; I didn't need my client's innocence competing with real-life human drama.

"How well did you know Carol Phillips?" asked the deep voice.

"I just met her last night, but I know her brother quite well."

"Parker Phillips? The man they've arrested?"

"Yes. I'm his lawyer."

"So you don't believe he killed his sister."

"Certainly not. After a very sloppy and cursory investigation, the police have developed a case that depends on coincidence and exotic flights of imagination. In their haste to make an arrest, they've overlooked several important factors that I am now investigating myself."

"Will you tell us what those factors are?"

"The identity of the murderer, for one."

"Does that mean you know?"

"I didn't say that."

"Do you think Phillips will be charged?"

"That depends on whether the district attorney will be able to look at the facts coolly and methodically, or whether he will succumb to the hysteria that seems to pervade the San Francisco Police Department."

"Thank you, Miss Schwartz."

Now that it was over, I had second thoughts. Ninety-nine out of a hundred lawyers would have gone the "no-comment" route. But my dad always said that the most important ingredient for being a good lawyer was a generous portion of ham. I didn't see that I'd done any harm, anyway; I'd twitted the cops, and maybe I'd be giving the murderer a flutter—he'd be sure to watch the news.

As I fumbled for my keys, one of the pad-and-pencil fellows ambled up. I'd noticed him already. He wasn't exactly handsome, but he had fabulous electric blue eyes and a quality of vitality, of energy about him that attracted me. He said he was Rob Burns from the *Chronicle*. Instantly, I was on my guard. "Can I see your press card?"

He grinned. "Sure. You know, you're only the second

person who's ever asked me that. Journalism ain't what it used to be.''

The card looked okay. "I don't understand," I said. "The *Chronicle* doesn't publish on Sundays. Why aren't you out hiking on Mount Tam or something?''

"Aren't you clever! We *don't* work on Saturdays. I heard about the murder on the radio and called the city editor for a special dispensation. I knew I'd have to work on it tomorrow—for Monday's paper—so I didn't want to take a chance on missing you. You're the lawyer for HYENA, aren't you?''

I didn't deny it.

"I've seen you around. You were great on the Margaret Blythe Show. I've, uh, I've wanted to meet you for a long time." It is true that I'm a sucker for flattery, but lest you get the idea that I'm just a plain sucker, let me emphasize that he said it almost shyly. Delivery counts for a lot. I thought there was a good chance he might turn into an ally, so I didn't fight the initial attraction I'd felt.

"I've kind of had the illicit-sex beat lately," he continued. "In fact, I've covered some of your press conferences, and I covered the Strumpets' Strut. When I heard a Carol Phillips was found dead in the apartment of a Rebecca Schwartz, I remembered somebody I'd met at the, uh, Strut. Kandi Phillips. Now no one is named Kandi; it's the same woman, isn't it?''

"AKA," I said.

"San Francisco State student with an unconventional way of paying her tuition.''

"You're not going to use that?''

"She didn't have a rap sheet. I've already checked.''

"It's against the law for the cops to give out that information. . . .''

"Or for me to receive it." The blue eyes were deliciously naughty. "But they did, and I did, and since she's never been arrested, I don't see how I can say the lovely Kandi was a hooker, unless . . .''

"Unless you want me to sue your ass.''

"I'm not particular. I'd like anything you did with my ass."

"Do you have everything you need, Mr. Burns?"

"Rob. There's only one thing. There's been a lot of mob activity lately."

"What do you mean?"

"I can't be specific yet. Just a lot of pushing and shoving, kind of establishing territory. I don't really know what it's all about, but I can't help wondering if they're trying to move in on prostitution in the area. It's all independent now, as you know."

"So what does that have to do with this?"

"That's what I wanted to ask you. Is is possible Kandi was somehow involved with them and got in too deep?"

Now that was an idea. But I discarded it after a few moments' thought. "I don't see how. This wasn't what you'd call your 'execution-style' murder. Remember, she was bludgeoned to death. The cops might not have told you, but my apartment was ransacked as well. That doesn't smack of mob work."

"Sure doesn't. Well, you can't blame a guy for trying. I'm glad I got to meet you, anyway. I hope it isn't for the last time."

He closed his notebook and left with a wave.

CHAPTER 10

When I'd come back from Mickey's earlier that day, I'd been so hopped up on coffee and so much looking forward to getting out of those horrid clothes that I must have had a false sense of well-being. Now, as I entered my ravaged apartment, waves of despondency engulfed me like a soggy towel. You know how I feel about my apartment. It was violated. It was raped and pillaged. And so I felt that I was.

But I am a naturally sanguine person, and that is no accident. I work at it. I learned a long time ago that the best cure for melancholy is action. Clawing frantically at the soggy towel, I pawed through my records until I found an album of Strauss waltzes, a proven nostrum for whatever-ails-you. I put it on, got into jeans, and put the place back together.

Practically everything had been thrown off the shelf in the hall closet, and the drawers there and in my bureau had been rummaged, though not too badly. The same went for the kitchen. As I worked, I saw that my initial impression had been right; it was really a very cursory job of ransacking. But it was logical. It was the sort of quick blitz you might have made if you were really looking for something, rather than trying to prove somebody'd been looking for something. No mirrors were broken for dramatic effect; nothing was knocked over for no reason at all. I was more convinced than ever that it was a genuine search.

After I'd satisfied my rage for order, I applied Spic and

Span to the fingerprint powder, and it worked nicely. Remember that in case you ever need to know it, God forbid.

I had to work up to calling Parker's parents. Nobody wants to tell perfect strangers their son is in jail for killing his sister. So I called Chris instead. She never listens to the radio, and anyway, I wouldn't want her to hear about the murder that way. Halfway through my narrative, she bummed a cigarette from Larry, breaking a six-month-old vow.

She thought the impromptu press conference was a bad move, but promised to watch it anyhow.

I called my dad to see what he thought. My mom answered: "Rebecca, thank God! Your father wants to talk to you. Are you all right, darling?"

I said I was, and Daddy came on the phone. "My daughter, the celebrity," he said. "Your name's all over the radio."

"Not as much as it's going to be. Daddy, did Mom tell you they've arrested a suspect? And that I'm his lawyer?"

"Yes." His voice was serious. "Are you sure you can handle it?"

"I think so. Listen, here's what I did. When I got home, every reporter in town was here. So I denounced the police department and made emotional protestations of my client's innocence. Do you think I went too far?"

He laughed—deep, rumbling, appreciative guffaws. "What's the harm? The worst that could happen is the D.A. could claim prejudice and ask for a change of venue if the case gets to trial. But what's the big deal? You're doing fine, *bubee*. You're your father's daughter."

"You'll watch, won't you?"

"Sure. Six o'clock?"

"I don't think so. More likely eleven."

There were no more ways to put it off, so I called Parker's folks. His mother answered. She didn't interrupt me as I identified myself as Parker's lawyer, explaining the position, and assured her there was nothing to worry about; the police didn't have a decent case, and I was sure he'd be released.

"I see," she said. Her voice trickled from the receiver

like ice water. "Are you sure he has competent legal counsel?"

Did I need that?

I counted to ten, quick, and didn't decide till I got to seven whether or not to let her get away with it. "Mrs. Phillips," I said finally, trying not to sound as icy as she had, "I know you've had several bad shocks today, so perhaps you aren't aware that you're being insulting."

"I beg your pardon," she said. "I didn't realize what I was saying. I suppose I had a snobbish urge for a—for someone well known. There is a criminal lawyer named Isaac Schwartz, I believe, who . . ."

"He's my father," I said.

"Oh. Well then. You must be with the same firm."

"No, but I'll see that Parker has the best advice I can give him. If he isn't satisfied, he can fire me. Fair enough?"

"Very well. Thank you for calling."

My hand shook as I put down the phone. Why had I admitted Isaac Schwartz was my father? Hoping a little of the glory would rub off on me? Bad form, Rebecca. And a thoroughly unpleasant encounter. I didn't know what ailed Mrs. Phillips, but I supposed she was either rich or well-born. One or both of these things sometimes makes for haughtiness.

I turned on the TV and didn't see myself. Then I went into the bathroom to start getting ready for dinner with Jeannette, pausing to squeeze the rug at the bottom and pluck a few more feathers off.

Jeannette always wanted to dine at the Washington Square Bar and Grill. As you may know, this is a North Beach hangout that has not won coast-to-coast acclaim for its fine food, but its clientele is supposed to be very "in." And since Jeannette was very "in," she liked to be seen there. The place is a plum-colored womb with white tablecloths, dark wood, and plenty of light, so everyone can see who's there.

I walked the five or six blocks from my house, preceding Jeannette by about five minutes. She bustled in, arms flying, making her purple cape a perpetual motion machine that slapped at passing waiters. "I simply cannot believe it about Kandi! We were all together not two hours before it must have happened, and then you . . ." She stopped, apparently to spare my feelings.

"You heard it on the radio?" I asked.

"Yes. Tell me everything."

"Let's sit down first. Did you make a reservation?"

She had. In moments, we were seated at a good table with a liter of white wine on the way. For the umpteenth time, I told my story. The wine came, and we both ordered petrale, and it came.

Jeannette was properly impressed with the yarn. When I had supplied every scarifying detail she asked for—except, of course, Senator Handley's identity—I asked about the proposition she'd mentioned the night before.

"It's this way," she said. "We need a lobbyist. We've been using one of our members, and she's been reasonably effective, but she wants out. She says the legislators don't take her seriously because she's been a prostitute. And furthermore, they expect her to put out. Can you beat that?"

"I'm not surprised."

She ignored me. "The stigma follows you for the rest of your life. No one ever thinks of you as Jeannette, with a mother and dad in Iowa, or Jeannette with a degree in English lit; they just think of you as Jeannette the prostitute. Does that seem fair to you?"

"It only makes sense. People think of me as a lawyer. So what?"

"It's another example of horizontal hostility. And male chauvinism as well."

"I think it's an act of male chauvinism for a legislator to proposition a female lobbyist, but I can also see the problem of getting him to take an ex-prostitute seriously. I'm sorry, Jeannette, but it's cultural bias and you're stuck with it."

"Well, that's what I'm getting to. We don't want to replace her with another member. How would you like the job?"

"What, you're not satisfied with my work?"

"We are very satisfied with your work. Otherwise, I wouldn't ask. You're well known and well respected. And we can trust you."

I shook my head. "No thanks. I'm one of those rare people who actually like their work. No sense taking any chances."

"That's what I thought you'd say, but it doesn't hurt to ask. Can you recommend anybody?"

"Not offhand. I'll give it some thought. Right now, I've kind of got my mind on other things. Would you mind if I pumped you about Kandi?"

"Not at all. Though I didn't know her very well, and from what I gather, that's just as well. She was a tramp."

I laughed. "Isn't that horizontal hostility?"

"No. *You're* exhibiting it. You just made it clear that you think a tramp and a prostitute are the same thing." She patted her neat publicist's coif, as if to emphasize her own respectability and worth. "There's an ethical code among prostitutes, which is very strongly adhered to by HYENA members."

"Kandi wasn't a member?"

"No. She wasn't a feminist. She didn't get along with other women at all. She was a kind of hanger-on, and she came to a couple of our meetings, but she actually laughed out loud if anyone mentioned the word 'sisterhood.' Used to say we were fools if we believed in it. And she made fun of Elena's co-op. I say 'Elena's' because it's easier, but I hope you understand that I don't think of it that way—Stacy and Renée and Hilary are just as much a part of it."

I nodded, to pacify her.

"No one liked her. But Elena kept her because she brought in a lot of business. She was very popular with the customers, although I suspect she had as much contempt for men as she did for her sisters."

I almost said I could see how the nature of the business

might easily breed that, but I thought better of it. Instead, I asked how often Kandi had worked at the co-op.

"Once or twice a week, I think. Even though she was popular, Elena was uneasy about her. After she started working there, she became the favorite of a couple of Elena's best clients. Influential men, well known in the community, who'd been clients of Elena's—I mean of the co-op's—for quite a while. They started asking for Kandi specifically, and then after a while they stopped going to Elena's."

"Elena thought that had something to do with Kandi? That she was driving them away?"

"Either that, or seeing them somewhere else, so she wouldn't have to split the money with Elena. That's what I mean by ethics. An ethical prostitute wouldn't do that."

"But you don't know for sure that it was that?"

"No. In fact, Elena thinks it may have been something worse. She may literally have been driving them away. By blackmailing them."

"Oh. So why didn't Elena get rid of her?"

Jeannette shrugged. "She didn't have any real basis for thinking that. It was just a feeling. Remember, Elena is a very shrewd businesswoman, and Kandi did bring in business. After all, it could have been a coincidence; maybe the clients had found someone they liked better at another house. So she decided to wait and see if it happened again. The three-strikes-and-you're-out theory."

Coffee had come, and I helped myself to cream and sugar. "How," I said finally, "did Kandi get the job at Elena's?"

"That's the ironic part. Through me, helping out a sister. Kandi came to HYENA in big trouble. Or what she thought was big trouble. She'd been working for an escort service run by somebody named George. But she started cheating him, taking his clients, the same way she may have been taking Elena's. George found out about it, called her up, and threatened to kill her.

"She was a mess when she came to me. George is a pretty

big operator in this town, and she knew it. She was new to the business, and she thought he might kill her.''

''Did you think so?''

She waved a scornful, well-manicured hand. ''Of course not. He was just being macho. I told her not to worry about it and gave her a stern lecture on ethics. She said she wasn't aware she was doing anything wrong. It was she the clients liked, and she didn't see why she shouldn't pocket the entire fee. I told her that wouldn't do at all, and she seemed very contrite, very willing to learn. You know those innocent kitten eyes of her. I fell for it. I knew Elena was looking for some part-timers, so I sent her over there. I told Elena the whole story, of course, but she seemed satisfied Kandi was reformed. Until she got nervous about losing the two clients.''

''What about this George? Was he at Elena's party?''

''I don't know, but he *could* be an FDO for all I know. I've never seen him. Rumor has it he's a respectable businessman who runs the escort service on the side.''

We'd dawdled over our coffee for a long time, so long that most of the restaurant's clientele had turned over once. Jeannette excused herself for a trip to the ladies' room.

From where we were sitting in the dining room, you could see through a large open doorway to the bar. Idly, I looked that way. A man I recognized stared back. It was Frank, the fellow I'd met at Elena's who'd wanted to call me Becky and negotiate an illegal transaction. He'd obviously been watching me.

Seeing his chance, he left the bar and came over to my table.

''Hi,'' he said. ''I nearly didn't recognize you. But everybody knows Jeannette von Phister. Since you're with her, I figured you had to be the lovely Rebecca, looking wholesome instead of exotic. That's quite a trick you've got. Not unappealing at all.''

I gave him my standard freeze line: a haughty ''What can I do for you?'' But I forgot it might sound different coming from a supposed prostitute than from a lawyer. He seemed to take it for an invitation: "I thought we might continue the conversation we started last night."

That was my cue to 'fess up to being a clean-living American girl. But for the second time that day I failed a test of character. Somehow it just seemed easier not to, especially since Jeannette was on her way back from the ladies' room. I flicked my eyes in her direction. "Perhaps," I said, "some other time."

"I'd like that," he said. "Maybe we could do a little business. I've been looking for someone like you."

He produced a business card and laid it on the table. It read "High-Life Escort Service" and gave a phone number. That was all. "Just ask for Frank," said Frank, nodding briefly to Jeannette as he walked away.

"Who is that man?" I asked her when she sat down again.

"Never saw him before in my life. I thought you knew him."

"He was at Elena's party last night." I looked at my watch. "I'd better go if I'm going to watch myself on television. Just one last question about Kandi. What was the name of that escort service she worked for?"

"I don't know. The Top Hat or something. No—I've got it. The High Life."

CHAPTER 11

I debated calling a taxi to take me home, but decided that was silly. It was only a few blocks, and the November air would do me good. Anyway, I was wearing my invincible black leather jacket ($250 at Saks). A walk would be a good opportunity to digest not only petrale, but information as well.

As I saw it, I had discovered three possible motives for killing Kandi. George, whoever he was, had been double-crossed by Kandi and had actually threatened her. And one of his agents had been at the party. Or maybe Frank was actually George; you never knew. No matter what Jeannette said, I imagined pimps, even high-class ones, might be dangerous. Maybe George felt he'd had to knock Kandi off to keep the rest of his women in line. Or maybe he'd just argued with her and lost his temper. Or maybe she'd stolen something from him and he was trying to get it back.

Or maybe he was in love with her: you always hurt the one you love.

Then there were the two clients who'd mysteriously cut themselves off from the lubricious ministrations of the co-op. If Kandi were blackmailing them, she was probably using some object as a threat, something to prove she had enjoyed an illicit liaison with the blackmailee. Letters were the usual thing, but I'd never heard of anyone writing incriminating letters to a prostitute. Still, you never know about people's sexual whims; look at Senator Handley's preferences.

It didn't have to be letters, though. Just some personal object: maybe an inexpensive and easily identifiable pen, a photograph—perhaps of the wife and kids themselves—lifted from the client's wallet, or some other piece of identification—even a driver's license. Who knew? Maybe a pair of silk monogrammed boxer shorts. I stopped myself. Now that really *was* ridiculous. Anyone would miss his undershorts.

Whatever it was, perhaps the influential person (either of them) had some reason to think Kandi had it with her that night and had killed her for it and then searched my apartment until he found it. But the problem was that he apparently *had* found it. That got me no closer to knowing what it was, which got me no closer to knowing where to look for it. I would just have to ask Elena for the clients' names, that was all, and see if I got any brilliant ideas when I had them.

Just to make sure I didn't overlook anything, I tried to think whether Jeannette had said anything that suggested a motive for either herself or Elena. But I was damned if I could put my finger on one. A pimp might kill a double-crosser, but would a madam? A feminist madam at that? Maybe I was being sexist, but I couldn't see it. I even considered whether Jeannette would kill her for giving the profession a bad name, but that was dumb. The *Chronicle* had once called Jeannette, much to her horror, "the suzerain of San Francisco's strumpets." It might have been tacky, but it was true. Jeannette would have had the power to see that Kandi never worked any lucrative house in San Francisco again. She didn't need to murder her.

I let myself into my apartment. This time it looked like home. I went straight to the bedroom, which is as light and airy and feminine as the rest of the place is modern and hard-edged, and I put on the old-fashioned white muslin night-gown Mickey had once made me for a birthday present. Then I poured myself a brandy and settled down on the rose satin comforter I inherited from my favorite Aunt Ellen and I turned on the eleven o'clock news.

Your honor may take judicial notice that the witness is prejudiced, but I thought I was terrific.

Sunday morning dawned as clear and crisp as the Saturday before it. At least I assumed it did. It was like that when I got up at ten.

I went downstairs, got the Sunday paper, and threw it on my bed. Then I made myself some bacon, orange juice, coffee, and two poached eggs on toast—done perfectly, if I say so myself. I arranged these delicacies artfully on one of those wicker breakfast-in-bed trays that you get at Gump's for about $100 (a gift from my parents) and carried it into the bedroom.

"Breakfast, Rebecca," I hollered cheerfully. "Rise and shine. Don't want your eggs to get cold."

"Oh, you sweet thing!" I answered. "You really shouldn't have. Just look at those eggs!"

Whoever said living alone is lonely? Gary only made me breakfast in bed on my birthday. Rebecca is *much* more solicitous.

I got back into bed with my tray and reached for the paper. In San Francisco, the Sunday paper is a kind of hybrid, the result of a merger some years ago between the *Chronicle* and the *Examiner*. The *Chronicle* became a morning paper, and the *Examiner* took the afternoon slot, with Sunday thrown in as a sop; the Sunday news sections, that is. What makes the paper a hybrid is that the *Chronicle* has certain sections in it: the comics, something called "The Sunday Punch," and a magazine offering.

You may wonder how I managed to restrain myself from reading the murder story before I made breakfast. I might not have if it hadn't been for the events of the day before—I mean telling Mrs. Phillips I was Isaac Schwartz's daughter and failing to tell Frank I wasn't a prostitute. I did it as a character-strengthening exercise. After those two lapses, I figured I needed it.

The *Examiner* had managed to dig up a picture of Kandi from somewhere—maybe from San Francisco State—so she smiled out at me from two columns on page one, looking like everybody's favorite homecoming queen. And guess whose Semitic mug occupied the adjacent two columns? Mine. The caption said, "Discovered body in her apartment," not "Attorney for the unjustly accused brother." But you can't have everything.

I guess someone took the picture at my al fresco press conference, because I was wearing my white silk blouse and coral necklace. It wasn't at all bad, and neither was the story, which was written by someone named Silvia Estevez. She got my quotes right and used the ones I cared about. And she didn't hint that Kandi had been anything other than a wholesome, innocent college student. Thank God for libel laws.

I perused the rest of the paper only superficially, allowing enough time to pass until I judged it was a decent hour to call Elena. This occurred at 11:45.

Elena had spent several grim hours with Martinez the day before, and she sounded beaten. "Parker had to tell who I am," she said. "So Martinez made me explain about the FDOs and give him the president's name, so I guess he'll go over the guest list, and I'll never get any of those people as clients. Not that I have anyplace to entertain them anymore. I've closed the house now that the cops know about it. Have to start looking for a new location tomorrow, but you can't move wallpaper and carpets. All that's down the drain. I'm still getting calls and parceling out tricks in hotels, if the clients are willing to spring for it, so we still have a little income. But even that makes me nervous. They probably have the phone tapped by now."

I murmured something flip about the wages of sin, but luckily Elena didn't hear it. Luckily because I remembered the whole quote: "The wages of sin is death." I changed the subject.

"Listen, Elena, you know that favor you owe me? I'm ready to collect. May I come over and ask you about a zillion questions?"

"Sure," she said resignedly. "Stacy's here—is that okay?"

I said it was.

Elena had left the curtains drawn. Gloom pervaded the house like a miasma. What had seemed so amusing a parody before was now a grisly mockery, in my eyes at least. But I don't think Elena would have put it quite so dramatically. She was more concerned with financial than aesthetic hardship.

The kitchen, at least, was still cheerful and was populated by Stacy, with whom I exchanged hellos. She, if you recall, was the tiny one who dressed like a little girl at the FDOs party. She was my client, of course, but I'd never known her well and never especially cared for her. She wasn't wearing make-up that day, and she looked about twelve—a hard, pinched, colorless twelve, with sharp little teeth.

Elena poured us all a fortifying tot of sherry and we sat around the kitchen table drinking it.

"As you know," I began, "I believe Parker is innocent. That means someone else must have killed Kandi. So the questions I'm going to ask are aimed at trying to find out who it might have been. Can you bear with me?"

Elena nodded. Stacy let her expression slide from bored to slightly contemptuous.

"Okay, what happened after I left the party?"

Stacy shrugged. "It fizzled."

"Elena?"

She ruffled her hair with her mandarin nails. "God, I was furious. As soon as I realized the raid was a phony, I started to worry about those blank shots, which really *could* have brought the police, despite the soundproofing." She stopped, snapped her fingers, and looked glum.

"What's the matter?" I asked.

"She's just remembered how much soundproofing cost," Stacy said. "And now it's no good to us. Shit!"

Elena snapped, "Stacy, do you have to talk like a streetwalker in front of Rebecca? Lighten up a little." She turned back to me. "Anyway, once I realized what those overaged adolescents were up to, all I wanted to do was get them and their tiresome boyish mirth off the premises, but it was only midnight and they'd rented the house till two o'clock. I didn't want a scene, of course—"

"Hell, no," said Stacy. "There was still a chance some of them might want to come back as customers."

"That was one reason," said Elena icily. "So I went to the president and told him I'd be happy to return a portion of the money, but I was sorry, they'd have to go, and would he make an announcement to that effect?"

"And?"

"He was a perfect gent." She looked at me. "He apologized for scaring away the piano player, even though he said he hadn't known about the prank, and he said the party was kind of dead without music. So he just announced it was over and asked everyone to leave as soon as they'd finished their drinks."

"How did the FDOs take it?"

"They seemed rather relieved. The raid unnerved them, I think. People started to drift away almost immediately, and everyone had left by a little after twelve-thirty."

"Let's face it, the party was a fiasco," said Stacy.

"How long did you and the other hostesses stay?" I asked her.

"About twenty minutes longer, I guess. As long as it took to pick up glasses and empty ashtrays, anyway. We weren't getting paid, so naturally everyone wanted to get home as soon as possible."

I was puzzled. "What do you mean, you weren't getting paid?"

"We—all the co-op members, I mean, which was everybody except Kandi—were going to split the thousand dollar fee for the party.'' She snorted. ''A big two-fifty apiece! We were so eager to get out, we had the place practically cleaned up by the time the last guest left.''

''Stacy never liked the idea of the party,'' Elena said, as if to explain the friction between the two women. I had an idea it was more than that, though. Stacy was impressing me more by the minute as a grasping little dodo, and I suspected Elena shared the opinion.

''Did Kandi leave with the others?'' I asked.

''She left with me,'' Stacy said. ''We found your purse when we were cleaning up, and Elena sent her to your house to return it. I live in North Beach—on the low-rent side of Telegraph Hill—so I asked Kandi to drop me off.''

''Why didn't Elena send the purse with you, then?''

''I don't even have a car, and I was tired and I wanted to go home. We didn't know if you'd be home or if someone would have to wait for you, or what.'' She gave it one last little self-righteous shot: ''Anyway, Kandi was still on duty.''

''How's that?''

''The senator plunked down five hundred dollars for the pleasure of greeting the dawn with her,'' said Elena. ''That meant half for the house and the other half for her. But he was gone, and I figured Kandi might as well do something to earn her two-fifty.''

''Besides,'' said Stacy, ''it was easier than fighting with me about it.'' Her voice was unmistakably malicious.

Elena sighed. ''You got it, honey.''

''It was a kind of special occasion for the senator,'' she continued. ''He spent the afternoon with Stacy and Kandi.''

''Wait a minute,'' I said. ''You mean the senator spent the afternoon with Kandi and Stacy, then wanted a whole night with Kandi? What kind of freaks have we got in Sacramento?''

''He has a thing about being recognized and, as you have no doubt gathered, very specific tastes. He would always come in the back door and have Kandi meet him in the kitchen, which of course was always locked when he was expected. She would be wearing a costume, a description of which I'll spare your middle-class ears, and she'd be holding a candle. Otherwise, the kitchen would be dark. We even have special window coverings for his visits.

"I believe he and Kandi had some sort of dialogue they had to go through, the gist of which was that he was Kandi's slave. Kandi would undress him, handcuff and blindfold him, and put him in that black robe you had the misfortune to see. Then she'd lead him downstairs to the 'torture chamber' and tie him up. Part of the deal was that he had to be left alone for long periods of time while Kandi was turning tricks. That was part of the 'torture,' if you see what I mean.

"She'd come back at intervals and do various entertaining things for him, some fairly conventional, some a bit on the imaginative side. That armoire is full of all sorts of things you don't want to know about. Anyhow, when we closed up for the night, he always left, because it ceased to amuse him if Kandi wasn't making it with other men between visits. A cool five hundred dollars every time."

"I thought you said something about greeting the dawn."

"The money covered that, but he never stayed past three o'clock."

"Go on."

"Well, he'd always wanted a session in the waterbed room with two women, but he never had the nerve to go upstairs when we were open for business. He tried to make his usual appointment for Friday, but I told him we'd be closed because of the party. He seemed to think that would be even more exciting than the usual routine—God knows why—and furthermore, since the house was also closed that afternoon, it meant he could go upstairs then. He offered me a hundred dollars each for Kandi and Stacy in the afternoon, then the usual five hundred dollars for the night." She shrugged. "That was nearly as much as we were getting for the whole damned party, and it meant I'd have Kandi as an extra hand at the party. The purpose of the party wasn't for the money—

one thousand dollars is about what we make in an hour on a good night—it was to get those FDOs interested in coming back as customers. And Kandi was quite a drawing card. So I didn't see how I could refuse."

"The little snit," said Stacy.

"Don't be jealous, dear," said Elena. "The senator specifically requested you for the afternoon."

Stacy showed her sharp little teeth. "I'm flattered as hell."

I changed the subject. "You two had better be careful the next time you give a party. If there's ever a real raid, you can't count on the lights going off so conveniently again."

Stacy whooped. Even Elena couldn't suppress a mild giggle.

"Did I say something?"

"My poor innocent," said Elena. "That's the only thing we *can* count on. Didn't you think it was a hell of a coincidence? I just flipped a little switch under the mantel."

"Oh." I was so put out I asked a question I already knew the answer to. "How'd the FDOs know about your place, anyway, if they weren't customers?"

"I told you that when I called you. Jeannette arranged it."

"Unfortunately," said Stacy. She just couldn't leave well enough alone.

It occurred to me that Jeannette had done quite a bit of arranging: first the job for Kandi, then the party. Did that mean anything? Probably not. She could hardly have predicted Kandi was going to wind up alone at my house. No one could, for that matter; it didn't seem to be a premeditated murder.

The phone rang, affording me a glimpse of a side of Elena I hadn't seen. She made her voice low and inviting: "Well, heLO, dear. I've been hoping you'd call." Bawdy giggles. "What a MARvelous idea. You're so inVENtive, darling. I'm getting excited just talking to you. Darling, there's only one problem. I'm having a little work done on the house right now. How about a hotel, hm? Wouldn't that be fun for a change? All right, dear. I can hardly wait."

She replaced the receiver, muttered "asshole" and poured us some more sherry.

"He speaks very highly of you," I said.

"Oh, he's all right," she said as she made a notation in an appointment book. "I'm just fed up right now, that's all. In fact, I'm sick and tired of phone calls." She took the receiver off the hook. "There. What else do you want to know?"

"Has the senator come for his clothes yet?"

"Oh dear, didn't I tell you? He called about ten minutes after you drove away with him. What happened, anyway?"

"He abandoned ship when I hit that car. I guess he must have panhandled a dime." I giggled at the notion.

"Anyway," said Elena, "he said he had to get his clothes right away. Jeez, he really had a thing about being discovered."

"The cops don't give a shit for johns," said Stacy. "Especially if they're influential.

"True," said Elena, "but we had to indulge him. I told him it wasn't really a raid and that I could put his clothes in the basement so he could get them by coming in through the tunnel. The armoire can be moved from either side, you see."

"When did you do it?"

"Right away. I mean, I asked Kandi to. I was pretty busy with the FDOs. I presume she did and that he came back for them, because they weren't here the next morning."

"So he was here later on. He's as good a suspect as anybody."

Stacy snickered. "Suspect! Who do you think you are— Miss Marple?"

I lost patience. "Stacy, I wish you wouldn't needle me while I'm trying to do my job."

"Okay, okay."

"Did you tell the senator he had to tell the cops he was here?" I asked Elena.

"Yes, and he said he would. Amid much shouting and

hysteria. I had to leave a message with his answering service, which wasn't cool."

"Good." I turned to Stacy. "On the ride home with Kandi, did you notice anyone following you?"

"I wasn't looking in the rearview mirror."

"But Kandi was. Did she mention anything like that?"

"No. All she mentioned was, she was pissed off she had to go clear to Telegraph Hill and wait for you."

She showed her teeth again, as if she were delighted to have said something personally offensive.

"Okay, look," I said, "does either of you know of anyone with a motive to kill Kandi?"

"Only everyone," said Stacy.

"She means," said Elena, "that Kandi was such a pain that most anyone might have wanted to wring her lovely neck. But real motives, no, so far as I know."

"Stacy?"

"No."

"Well, how about alibis—did either Renée or Hilary leave with anybody?"

Both women shook their heads. "They left separately, before Kandi and I did," said Stacy. "Even before Elena asked Kandi to return your purse, so they didn't know where she was going. But of course they could have waited, and followed her. Elena's the only one with an alibi."

"How did you get that?"

"She was picking you up at the Hall of Injustice. And that makes me the most likely suspect, since I'm the only one besides her who knew where Kandi was headed." Her voice was bitter.

"She could have stopped by my place on the way," I said. If I hoped to get a guilty reaction, I was disappointed. Stacy continued looking sulky. Elena only laughed.

"So no one has an alibi," said Elena. "Not even me or Jeannette or the senator. Where does that get us?"

"I'm not sure. But let me try something else on you. The

night of the party, did either of you meet a guy named Frank? Big, beefy guy—kind of red-faced?''

Both said no. Stacy looked at her watch. "I gotta go," she said. "Got a date. Thanks for the sherry and all that."

"What's with her?" I asked when she was gone.

"Oh, she's not such a bad sort. We're just annoyed with each other at the moment.

"She was one of those kids who got batted about from foster home to foster home, and I guess she grew up poor and unloved. So she got married at sixteen to some older guy who was going to save her, but it turned out he beat her. She left him and a series of dreary file clerk jobs until someone propositioned her and she learned how to make easy money."

"So she's insecure about being poor and upset about having to close the house."

"Yes, and angry with me, but it's not serious. What she was doing here today was—well, seeking comfort, basically.

I still wasn't exactly in love with Stacy, but I did like Elena's maternal, tolerant attitude. She was much too fine a woman for a life of crime.

"I have to go myself," I said, "but I want to ask you one last thing." I hoped she'd had enough sherry to loosen her tongue.

I told her about my conversation with Jeannette; how I'd learned Elena thought Kandi might have been blackmailing clients; how I thought this might provide a motive for murder. Elena's eyes widened.

"So I'm going to ask you to give me their names," I finished quickly.

"No. Oh no. I can't give you the names of clients, even to you. My God, especially not these two. No. Christ. No. I just can't do it."

I thought about Jeannette's homily on ethics. You couldn't say Elena didn't live by the code. I respected her for it and said so. But I added this: "Listen, if push comes to shove with my client, I'll have to tell the police. And then they'll ask you."

"I understand," she said, nodding. "But look, Rebecca, aren't you kidding yourself? If Kandi was killed by someone she knew, she must have let him in. Now, why would she open the door to someone she'd been blackmailing? It must have been someone she knew well and trusted. And I can't think of a more likely candidate than her own brother."

The words sounded as if they were meant to hurt. But maybe they weren't. Maybe Elena just meant to wake me up. I forgave her.

CHAPTER 12

I left wondering where all that got me. I now had detailed and unwelcome insight into the sex life of a senator, and I had the senator himself for a suspect. But no motive for him. And no names for the two men who might have had motives. But wait a minute! If Kandi were blackmailing other clients, might she be blackmailing the senator? I decided against it. He might like torture games, but amorous flights of the imagination with a blackmailer were out of that realm. If she were shaking him down, he'd have dropped her like the other two did.

So far as I could see, I had only one solid piece of information: confirmation of the time Kandi left Elena's. Elena had said ten minutes of one, which more or less agreed with my estimate. That meant Parker must have arrived at my place much later than Kandi did.

I headed my gray Volvo toward Eighth and Bryant streets, and the Hall of Justice, but I noticed with surprise that I did it reluctantly. I wasn't eager to see Parker. My feelings for him were very confused. Trying to pin them down did no good; I felt like a sea anemone, reaching for something I couldn't grasp. I knew that I disliked the mother role I'd been forced into. Yet I felt guilty about that. Here was a human being in genuine trouble who needed me; I should have been glad to help. And I *was* glad, on one level; it was by all odds the most interesting case I'd ever had. But I didn't like being a support system; I distrusted it. I didn't know if Parker and

I would be able to resume our previous relationship when this was all over, and I didn't know if I wanted to.

My next shrink appointment was Wednesday. I'd have to sort it all out then.

Parker had shaved, but he was still looking pale, and his forehead seemed permanently creased. He held me for a long time. I can't explain it, but I felt rather used. We didn't really know each other well enough to be going through this together.

"I talked to your mom," I said when we broke the clinch. "We didn't exactly hit it off."

"I should have warned you. She has a tendency to behave like a dowager duchess."

"Yes, well. She cast doubt on my professional expertise. Seemed to think you'd be better off with one Isaac Schwartz for a lawyer."

"Your father?" Parker actually laughed. Perhaps the shock was wearing off and he was beginning to feel more himself. "I hope you gave her the well-known piece of your mind."

"I wasn't exactly the soul of politeness."

"Good for you."

I told Parker things were looking better, without going into much detail. I let him know about the times, of course, but I thought it better to spare him the nuances that cast Kandi in an unflattering light. He had had enough hurt on that score, and he was bound to be in for more eventually. He had good news for me, too; he'd decided to take the polygraph the next morning.

I left feeling better, feeling more as if I could depend on him to call on his inner resources and not expect to draw his strength from me.

In fact, I felt damn good. It was a beautiful day, and I was going to a party that night. Not just any party, either—a celebration of thirty years of marriage. An astounding accomplishment.

I had nothing to do but think of frivolity for the rest of the

day. Murder just wasn't on the program. It was a good afternoon for Scarlatti.

For once that weekend, my parking space was empty. A
good omen. I parked, went in, performed the now-familiar
rug-squeezing, feather-picking ritual, and settled down at the
piano. As my fingers tripped lightly over the Scarlatti, I
looked out my window at the financial district. The sun
glinted playfully on its windowpanes, seeming almost to keep
time with me, performing its own glad, baroque Sunday afternoon dance.

The dance slowed, though, as evening fell, and finally
stopped. I felt some sober Bach would be appropriate, though
better on an organ. "Toccata and Fugue in D Minor" was
just the thing. Sober, yes, but always accompanied by tingles
and goose bumps—the result, no doubt, of too many view-
ings of *The Phantom of the Opera*. Perhaps, even as I played,
someone else was playing the same piece, a few blocks
southwest at Grace Cathedral.

I have no idea what time Episcopalians hold evening ser-
vices, but for some reason that thought made me look at my
watch. It was 5:30, and Mickey was picking me up in an
hour. I just had time to read a bit and get ready.

The reading I did in the bathtub. That accomplished, I was
able to apply myself, clean of body and enlightened of soul,
to the fascinating details of my toilet.

This I did with much pleasure, though vanity is not something to which we intellectual, ambitious types are supposed
to aspire. Perhaps this quality of indulging myself in the for-
bidden is one of the reasons for my ambivalent attitude toward prostitution. In fact, I know it is. But be that as it may,
I am much better able to accept vanity in myself lately. Now
that I have done well in college and law school and am starting to make it in the professional world, I don't worry so
much that people will think me frivolous. I know that I can
cope, and I don't need to prove it by neglecting my appearance.

For this occasion, though, false eyelashes and carmine

lipstick were best forgotten. Just a little make-up, the sort that's supposed to make you look "natural," and a good fluffing-up of the workaday hairdo. That would do it.

No worry about selecting an outfit, either. That had been done weeks ago: a red embroidered Chinese-style dress that had to be worn with pants, owing to the authentic side-slits. I'd discarded the tight black ones that came with it, found some soft jersey in the right color, and talked Mickey into making me some red ones. The effect was unorthodox, but very gay in the old-fashioned sense of the word.

At 6:30, I looked out my window, saw no sign of Mickey's Volkswagen, and cursed myself. Mickey was invariably twenty minutes late. If I'd remembered that, I wouldn't have been sitting around crumpling up my new outfit. I was too impatient to read, and I was burned out on playing the piano. It wouldn't take twenty minutes, but I could water my plants.

After slipping on an apron to protect my dress, I filled my two-gallon watering can and emptied most of it on the potted palm. Moving on to the asparagus fern nearest the piano, I picked up the foliage to get the nozzle near the dirt and gave it the tag end of the two gallons. But it wasn't nearly enough, so I refilled the can and splashed it liberally. Absentmindedly, I picked up the foliage of the other fern, stuck the nozzle in, and looked down to make sure I had it aimed correctly. A good thing, too, because if I hadn't, I'd have defaced a bundle of United States currency, which is a crime. The nozzle was resting right on the bundle, which was snuggled down in the ceramic pot, nicely hidden when the foliage was in place.

CHAPTER 13

I was so excited my hand jerked and I nearly drenched the bundle after all, but I deflected the flow in time, and it splashed harmlessly on the floor—harmlessly because I wiped it up right away, even before I took the money out and counted it. I did another thing before I handled the money: I put on gloves. Here, clearly, was the key to Parker's release and possibly to the identity of the murderer. I didn't want to risk smearing any fingerprints.

There was $25,000 in that bundle. People had killed for a lot less. I was sitting there with the money in my lap, trying to put things together in my head, when I became aware of a petty annoyance somewhere outside—the persistent honking of a horn. I didn't know how long it had gone on, but I knew what it meant. Mickey.

Brought abruptly back to the real world, I practically panicked. For a few minutes I'd completely forgotten I was all dressed up and expected somewhere special. But when I thought about it, there was only one thing to do. There are few matters so pressing they could divert me from calling the cops immediately when I've just found a suspicious small fortune—well, a year's salary, anyway—hidden in a flowerpot, but my parents' thirtieth anniversary was one of them.

In retrospect, I realize I could have just taken the money to the cops and driven my own serviceable Volvo to the party, arriving not more than an hour late. But at the time it seemed an either-or decision—the cops or the party. It had to be the party. I am nothing if not a good and dutiful daughter.

I waved at Mickey to stop her infernal leaning on her horn. Then I realized I still had a problem. To take the money or leave it? The solution presented itself almost at once. No one with any sense walks around with $25,000 in her purse. For three days now, the bundle had eluded the murderer, the police, and me just by hunkering down in a flowerpot. There was no reason why it shouldn't spend a few hours more there.

My coat and purse were already lying across the back of one of the sofas, so I had only to replace the money and gather them up. I was in Mickey's car not thirty seconds after making the decision.

"About time," she said. "There's a creepy guy in that car." She pointed to an undistinguished car parked on the curb in front of her '66 Valiant. All I could see was the back of someone's head.

"How do you know?" I asked, fumbling with the seatbelt. "You can't see him."

"Well, he's just sitting there for no reason at all. And I did see him when I drove up. He looked around."

She started the car, and as we drove around the vehicle, I looked over. The man had put his hand to the side of his face, ever so casually, blocking it from view. But I did see something interesting: a hook on the visor above the passenger seat.

I burst out laughing. "My dear girl, I'm under surveillance. That's a police undercover car. Look at the hook."

But Mickey was concentrating on her driving. "What hook? I didn't see anything."

"The hook on the visor; it's to hang a red light on, in case there's an emergency and the cop has to blow his cover to get through traffic. Now what the hell do the cops think I'm up to?"

But I was feeling too giddy to care. I vaguely noticed the other car swing into motion behind us, and then I forgot about it. Let them follow me to Timbuktu, I thought, if that's in their jurisdiction. It couldn't do any harm.

I gave Mickey an approving once-over. She had on a midnight blue dress with long sleeves, a sharp-pointed collar, and tailoring that made it cling like a natural integument. Her hair was gathered into a decorous coil on top of her head, an effect that conspired with prim pearl earrings to make a lady out of her.

"Last Living Hippie Burns Jeans, Joins Military-Industrial Complex," I said. "Tell me, Miss Schwartz, where have all the flowers gone?"

She giggled. "You don't look so bad yourself."

"After you, Alphonse. Listen, I've got $25,000."

"*Mazel tov.* Been to the track?"

"You're as bad as your boyfriend. I just found it. In my asparagus fern."

"Which one? And what have you been smoking?"

"The one near the . . . *Mickey!* Are you paying attention?" The light, as they say, dawned. Her paranoia about the undercover cop, her seeming inability to be serious . . . She was the one who'd been smoking.

"You're stoned, aren't you?" I said.

"Ummm." She smiled. "Half a joint left, if you want it."

I considered briefly, then decided against it. Very poor idea with that police car on our tail. "No," I said. "But listen, get straight, will you?" Mickey can do this when she wants to.

"Okay," she said. "Please tell me in plain English how it is that you have struck it rich. If you continue to insist that money grows in flowerpots, I shall consider it my privilege to be as whimsical as I please."

I spelled it out for her.

"Jesus Christ!" she said. "That's what the murderer was looking for!"

"Apparently."

"So what's your theory?"

I sighed. "I wish I had one. The only thing that makes sense is that Kandi stole it from someone at the party who followed her to my house and killed her for it."

"As theories go, it sounds okay to me." We rolled onto the Golden Gate Bridge.

"I wish you were thinking straight," I said. "There's one gigantic flaw in it: who in God's name would bring $25,000 to a whorehouse?"

Mickey giggled some more. She seemed to enjoy the idea enormously, but I was plain cross. "What's so funny about that?" I demanded.

"Oh, but you poor fool," she gasped. "You sure you don't want some dope to clear your head? Nothing could be more obvious." More inane giggles. I waited.

"Don't you see?" she said at last. "No one brought it there. It was already there."

"You mean she took it from Elena?"

"Of course."

"Mickey, you really are exasperating. What is that stuff anyway?"

She shrugged. "I don't know. Colombian something. Why not Elena?"

"It's the same problem. Who would have $25,000 lying around with 120 strangers in the house?"

"Oh." That stopped her. "I see what you mean. Elena isn't exactly scatterbrained, is she?"

I shook my head.

"I know," she said. "How about the fancyass client tied to the bed?"

"So far as I know, he isn't rich. Just influential. I don't even know where he'd *get* $25,000. And, again, he wouldn't be dumb enough to take it to a cathouse.

"Come to think of it, though, Kandi had a good chance to take it if he had. Elena said he came back for his clothes, and she'd had Kandi take them down to the basement. Kandi might very well have patted the pockets to make sure everything was there, discovered the money, and lifted it. Which would be perfectly safe because he didn't know she was the one who moved his clothes. Elena told him she was going to do it herself.''

"So he wouldn't know Kandi had it," said Mickey, "and therefore couldn't have killed her for it. And furthermore, as you've previously pointed out, he didn't have that kind of money and wouldn't have brought it there if he did.''

I groaned. "These are deep waters, Watson.''

We were silent for a while, and my thoughts lightly turned to blackmail. Surely $25,000 was much too big a chunk for even Kandi to blackmail anyone out of—at one time, anyhow. But even assuming she had, it didn't explain anything. A blackmailee wouldn't just hand a wad like that over and then kill to get it back. Blackmailers got killed, sure, but not in those circumstances. If you were going to kill someone to stop her blackmailing you, you could just skip the charade of the last payment.

Mickey and I were now climbing into the hills of Marin County, where my parents live. I hadn't seen the undercover police car for quite a while, and it wasn't behind us anymore.

In case you are not familiar with California, I will tell you that Marin is the richest county in the state. It is the ultimate suburbia, because there you can have the convenience of being only a few minutes from San Francisco and the luxury of not having a neighbor in sight. The houses are built on large, frequently vertical lots along narrow, winding roads, and the lots are overgrown with redwoods and eucalyptus so that the nearby houses are blocked from view. You can walk your grounds and pretend to be a country squire; you can see rabbits and raccoons; you can let your cats and dogs run freely; your children need not play in traffic. But if you cough loudly, your neighbors will hear and arrive with chicken soup—or, more likely, with some nostrum from a health food store. It is a place where, if you can afford it, you can have a good many things both ways.

My parents live on one of these winding roads, but their lot is nearly level. Their house is redwood and modern. The

rooms are large, and windows are plentiful. Sliding glass
doors across the back of the house open onto an indecently
large deck. The evening was warm, so the party would
doubtless spill out onto it.

One of the few hardships of life in Marin County is the
parking problem, but the denizens manage to keep a stiff
upper lip. Mickey found a parking place about a quarter of a
mile from the house.

As we walked to the party, I was grateful it wasn't raining.
I was wearing my wicked-woman shoes again, and they'd
had about all the encounters with puddles they could take.

Mom met us at the door, looking handsome in a black
dress. One thing I'll say for Mom; even though she was still
young when her hair started to gray, she didn't fight it. It's
coarse hair, and it turned a lovely silver, not white, with a
black streak or two. I'd say it's her best feature.

She kissed us and we "mazel toved" her. We did the
Alphonse-Gaston routine about our various outfits. "How's
Alan?" Mom asked Mickey. "I'll never forgive him for
missing our party." But she would. Alan had the one ac-
ceptable excuse: a performance with a small, poverty-stricken
theater group—which was as close as he ever got to gainful
employment. We Schwartzes may be Jewish, but we are very
big on the Protestant ethic.

Mickey said Alan was fine and working hard. I smirked
at both descriptions and Mom gave me a "tut-tut" or something close to it. My folks seem to like Alan, perhaps merely
because he is Jewish. That gets you a long way with some
families.

It was a good thing Alan wasn't there because he would
have been eaten up with jealousy. Like all actors, he likes to
be the center of attention, but there wasn't a chance that
night. Not with me there. There wasn't a person at the party
who hadn't seen me on page one of the paper that morning,
and precious few of them had missed me on TV. And there
must have been three hundred people there.

I didn't know Mom and Dad had so many friends. There

was the usual gaggle of relatives and old family friends, who kept pinching Mickey and me on the cheek and calling us *"shana madeleh."* But there were tons of people I didn't recognize, and some I knew from other contexts.

In fact, it was rather a star-studded gathering: several local politicians, from San Francisco as well as Marin; some rather fancy folk from what is sometimes called "the business community"—toilet-paper satraps, hotel suzerains, well-known investors—but, refreshingly, no pimps or whores that I recognized.

A thing I couldn't help noticing was that, in this older crowd, most of the achievers were men. Not all—there was Betty Blaine, one of the county supervisors—but most by far. So I felt perfectly justified in playing up my little celebrityhood. It kind of balanced things.

If I had a dollar bill for every time I told my story that night, I could take a week off and go to Mexico. I was on my third drink, and rather relieved when Daddy came along and insisted I eat something. Much more of that nonsense and I would have fallen on my face.

Daddy looked reasonably presentable that night. He is a short man with good white hair, as opposed to Mom's elegant silver, and he wears it collar-length. He has a fine hook nose that doesn't make him look harsh, probably because his light blue eyes are always joking. Unlike the rest of us, he is fair. And unlike the rest of us, he affects clothing that seems to come out of "free boxes" at Berkeley communes. His pants are always too short, and brown if his socks are gray, gray if they're brown. His suit jackets are two sizes too big, his shirts are always rumpled, and he generally sees to it that several grease spots are arranged artfully on his ties. Mom complains, but he says it's good for jury sympathy. Establishes his credentials as a *folks-mensh* or something. All this probably has something to do with my feelings about personal vanity, but I don't know what, exactly. If you want to know the truth, I think it's cute. He *is* a *folks-mensh*, so he may as well look like one.

That night he had on a dark blue suit—not expensive, but not aggressively ill-fitting, either—and a light blue shirt. I told him he was the handsomest man at the party.

"I should be, darling," he said. "I'm the youngest. Come and eat."

Like the obedient daughter I am, I followed him through the buffet line. My parents had gone all out. There was everything from chopped liver to fried wonton to poached salmon. I avoided most of the salads and took a lot of meaty things, on the theory that protein would keep me from getting drunk.

It was warm enough for the deck if you had a couple of drinks in you, so we headed out there.

"How's it going, Beck?" Daddy asked, and I knew I was in for trouble. He is the only person in the world allowed to use that childhood nickname, and only under conditions of the most egregious seriousness. Even he had better not mess with "Becky" or "Becca."

Wary, I asked, "How is what going?"

He stopped nibbling at a wonton. "The case."

"You haven't told me how you liked my TV performance."

He shook his head. "I worry."

"What, you didn't like it?"

"You didn't tell me you implied you knew who the killer was."

"So?"

"So it could be dangerous. Maybe the killer believes you; he goes after you next."

"Oh come on, Daddy."

"Beck, I think you're in over your head. I want you to turn it over to me."

I felt tears swim in my eyes, tears of rage and disappointment. My father, of all people!

"That's what Parker's mother wants me to do too. Nobody west of the Rockies seems to think I'm grown up or capable of doing a damn thing for myself!"

I put my plate down, preparing to flounce away in a swirl of righteous indignation. But Daddy caught my arm, and I looked at him. There were tears in his eyes, too. "*Bubee*, it isn't that. Your mother didn't sleep last night."

"She's got to learn I'm not a little girl anymore."

He patted my arm. "I know, darling. I'm sorry. I just don't want you to get hurt, that's all. Will you forget I said anything?"

"Okay," I said. But I said it sulkily.

"Rebecca?"

"Yes?"

"If it helps any, I'd feel the same way if you were a boy."

Oddly enough, it did help. Parents, after all, will be parents. "Daddy, will you tell me something honestly?" He nodded.

"Don't you think I'm a good enough lawyer to know when I'm in too deep? Don't you think I'd call you in a minute if I thought I couldn't handle it, or Chris couldn't?"

He considered for a few moments. Then he raised his eyes and looked straight at me. "You're an excellent lawyer, Rebecca. Maybe a little inexperienced, a little bit rash . . ." He shrugged. "But you would not hurt your client by taking on something you couldn't do. I have never seen your considerable arrogance get in the way of your judgment."

I laughed, because everything was all right again. "Arrogant, am I? Well, let me tell you something; if it goes to trial, God forbid, I'm going to need help."

"I know."

"Will you come in as co-counsel?" He squeezed my hand and nodded.

It was a decision I'd made from the first. I knew I couldn't let Parker's safety ride on my narrow experience. Or, for that matter, on the impaired judgment of a person who was emotionally involved with him. But I was still hoping it wouldn't go to trial.

My appetite was back, so I went in to get some cake. Mom caught me this time. She didn't say anything. She just engaged my glance, letting me know she couldn't look at me without tears in her eyes. I was damned if I'd let her get away with it.

"Take it easy, Mom," I said. "I'm going to be all right, and so is my client."

"Rebecca, tell me the truth."

"Okay."

"She was a whore, wasn't she? This, this . . . Carol Phillips?"

"Yes."

The tears overflowed, and I told her not to cry on her anniversary. "Don't worry, Mom. It doesn't rub off. Nobody's going to think . . ."

She was shaking her head violently. "No, no, no. You don't understand. I knew her. Her name was Kandi."

CHAPTER 14

It had to be right, Kandi's picture had been in the paper, but her professional name hadn't. That meant Mom must have known her, an occurrence about as likely as Kandi's membership in Hadassah—or Mom's in HYENA. I stood there like an idiot, waiting for it to sink in.

"I mean, I met her," Mom said. "At Walter's."

Ye gods. My uncle Walter. Mom's brother. Aunt Ellen's widower. Jeez, moneez. Uncle Walter was the success in the family. Dad was famous, sort of, but Uncle Walter was rich. He was an investor—in just about everything. How the hell could he have known Kandi? But I knew the answer, and it lay like a lump in my stomach.

"Home or office?" I asked shakily.

"Office. We were going to have lunch, Walter and I, and I was waiting for him to get off the phone. His secretary had already gone to lunch, so there was no one in the outer office. That's how she got in."

"Kandi, you mean."

"Yes. She poked her head in and gave him a big wink before she saw me. He got off the phone fast, acting very flustered, and asked what he could do for her. She said she'd just dropped in to see if he was free for lunch, and he said he wasn't; he even said he was having lunch with me and introduced us, very pointedly not asking her to join us.

"Then he said he'd see her out, and he kind of grabbed her arm."

"Affectionately?"

"No. Roughly. Your own uncle Walter! And I heard him tell her not to come to his office again. So naturally I asked him who she was. He said she was just a young woman he'd been giving some financial advice to, and he kept acting embarrassed and sheepish all through lunch."

"Well, I can see why you would have thought he was dating her, but what made you think she was a prostitute? He could have just been embarrassed because she was so young."

"I just knew, that's all."

"Come on, Mom."

"Well, I didn't really know for sure until I saw her picture in the paper and put that together with where you'd been the night she was killed. But that day in the office—" her voice got teary—"I knew she wasn't a real girl friend. I knew she didn't love him at all. I could see it in her face. You know what I could see? I could see malice. She enjoyed it, Rebecca. Embarrassing him like that."

From what I knew about Kandi, that didn't surprise me.

"Does Dad know about this?" I asked.

"No, and . . ."

"Don't worry, I won't tell him."

"This thing is much bigger than you think, Rebecca. You've got to get out."

I said I'd think about it, and I meant it.

I shivered, thinking of Elena refusing to tell me who the blackmailed—or *maybe* blackmailed—clients were. *"I can't give out the names of clients, even to you. My God, especially these two."* If Walter were one of them, could she have known he was my uncle? That would explain the "especially," but then lots of things might explain it.

At least this much was clear: Uncle Walter knew Kandi and may have been telling the truth about giving her financial advice. I knew from my experience with the HYENA members that prostitutes who were starting to make money frequently leaned on successful clients for that kind of advice. That would explain a visit to Uncle Walter's office.

But I could *not* convince myself that Uncle Walter could have had anything to do with the murder. My own uncle would not walk into my apartment and bash someone's brains out on the living room rug. It was simply not worth investigating.

I looked for Mickey, hoping she hadn't smoked the half a joint she'd offered on the way over. And ran straight into Uncle Walter. I kissed him and said wasn't it a lovely party.

He put his hands in his pockets and seemed to look straight through me. "Yes, darling, lovely," he said absently. Uncle Walter never uses words like "lovely."

"You're, uh, quite the celebrity, aren't you?" he said. Beads of sweat moistened his hairline.

I tried to put him at ease. "Hollywood's been calling all day," I said. "But don't worry; I won't forget my old friends."

"That's nice, dear. How's Alan?" He withdrew one of his hands and looked at his wrist. But there was no watch on it— only a band of skin lighter than the rest of his arm.

"Uh, fine," I said. "I guess. I haven't seen him in a couple of days."

He flushed, then tried out a smile. It came out a grimace. "Oh, you girls and your boyfriends. For some reason I confused you with Mickey."

I told him I thought he needed a drink, and offered to get it. "No thanks, dear," he said. "I'll get it myself." And he was off.

You don't know my uncle Walter, so you'll have to take my word for it that he was the most solicitous uncle anyone could have. He was the kind of uncle who not only remembered his nieces' birthdays, but also their boyfriends'. And sent the presents to the right address, too. Or more likely, hand-delivered them in his Mercedes.

I'd never seen him like that, never known him to confuse me with Mickey, or Alan with Gary—never, never had him brush me off. I had to face the fact that that was what he had done. To me, his favorite niece! There had to be a reason for it, but I wasn't sure I wanted to know what it was.

Dad spoke, at my elbow. "Rebecca, I want you to meet somebody you've got a lot in common with. Another friend of the downtrodden prostitute."

I extended my hand, holding back the words that sprang to mind: "Hello, Senator, I didn't recognize you with your clothes on." For it was Senator Calvin Handley.

At *his* elbow was his wife Josephine, who asked me almost immediately to call her Jodie. She had one of those never-a-hair-out-of-place coiffures, like Betty Ford, and she was wearing an Adolfo dress. She had something of Mrs. Ford's energy and vitality, too. I liked her right off, and felt sorry for her as well. She was the perfect political wife and then some, yet her husband had spent his Friday nights with Kandi Phillips. Probably told her he was tied up at the office, I thought, suppressing a giggle. Half of it was true, anyway.

"I feel as if I already know you," she said warmly. "I've been following your career ever since you became the lawyer for HYENA. In fact, Cal and I saw you on TV last night, didn't we, Cal?"

The senator nodded, beaming. He didn't seem a whit ill at ease.

"You know," continued Jodie, "I'm an honorary member of HYENA myself. I got on the bandwagon long before Cal did."

The senator might be used to duplicity, but it was driving me nuts. I hoped it didn't show in my face. "Oh?" I asked weakly. "How did you get involved?"

"I'd been actively working for the Equal Rights Amendment, and I've also been a longtime opponent of anti-abortion laws. I guess I must have been on some mailing list or other. They sent me a letter and asked me to attend one of their meetings."

"So you're a feminist."

"Of course." She smiled at her husband. "I was long

before the women's movement, and so was Cal. We've always had a very sharing sort of marriage.''

The senator's face was serious. ''I wouldn't say that, Jodie. Being married to a politician, you've had to endure a lot of—what's the Yiddish for trouble and woe, Rebecca?—*tsuris?*''

''Well, we've tried, anyway,'' said Jodie, not denying it. ''And Cal, as you know, has been very good about supporting feminist issues in the senate. But I like to think I had some influence with him on this bill to legalize prostitution.''

Since I had my doubts about the thing as a feminist issue, I asked Jodie her thoughts on the subject. ''I *do* agree with the HYENA arguments,'' she said. ''I'm sure many women turn to prostitution because of, well, misfortunes that make it impossible to make a living in a more conventional way.'' She looked vague for a moment. ''Lack of educational opportunities, children to support . . . But I must admit I support it on practical grounds more than anything. I think that's what finally convinced Cal I was right.''

''How do you mean?'' I asked.

''Well, it *is* the oldest profession, after all. Hundreds of years of prohibitions against it have failed to wipe it out. You may as well legalize it so you can regulate it, like marijuana.''

The senator smiled, still showing no sign of discomfort. ''Wait a minute, Jodie. Let's not get carried away.'' To me he said, ''Jodie's a little more advanced on the marijuana issue than I am. If she had her way, you could buy it in cigarette machines.''

''I understand that day is coming,'' I said. ''Or at least that the cigarette companies think it is. Supposedly they're all set to start producing twenty-joint packs as soon as it's legalized. But prostitution's a little different. It could so easily come under mob control.''

''But that's not the issue,'' Jodie insisted. ''Of course it could, but I don't think I care much who runs it. The mob is in a lot of legitimate businesses these days. Should we outlaw

Italian restaurants because they may be owned by the Mafia? Anyway, I'm not sure the mob is so much worse than the oil companies—or the cigarette people for that matter.''

''My dear!'' said the senator. His eyes twinkled at both of us. ''So now you know about the skeleton in the Handley closet,'' he said to me. ''I'm married to a firebrand radical.''

''A woman after my own heart,'' I said, and meant it.

Jodie smiled. ''Oh, there's Betty Blaine,'' she said. ''I've got to talk to her about something. Will you excuse me a moment?''

She fluttered gracefully away, energy and good nature fairly seething from her pores.

''At last we are alone,'' said the senator in a stage whisper.

''Again,'' I said.

''Yes. I think we'd better have a little talk, don't you?''

''Absolutely.''

''Good. How about my car?''

We walked out the back sliding doors, because they were closest, and around the house. Apparently he'd been able to get a parking place when someone else left, because he wasn't parked nearly so far away as Mickey and I. He opened the door of a tan Mercedes to let me slip inside. While he walked around to the other side, I inhaled the odor of newness and thought resentfully that it was a pretty fancy car for a man of the people.

He waited a moment to see if I'd speak first, but I didn't. ''I want to thank you for the other night,'' he said, ''and to apologize for my idiotic behavior. I didn't know who you were at the time, of course.''

''You were upset,'' I said.

''Upset! It's the worst thing that's ever happened to me.'' He looked at me with an appealing earnestness. ''Would you believe it if I told you I love my wife?''

''Yes. Anyone would love her.''

''You know far too much about me, my girl.''

My neck prickled. ''Is that a threat?''

The senator smiled and patted my hand. ''Good God, no!

I was admitting my own embarrassment, that's all.'' He became serious again. "I hope you can understand. I don't completely, myself, but I think it's something to do with power, something about guilt . . .''

"That makes you . . . made you go to Kandi, you mean?''

"Yes. I've done some reading on it, and I don't think it's too unusual. In fact, I started going after reading up on it, if you can believe that. You see, in my job, so much is at stake. One compromises so much, and there is so much corruption everywhere. . . . I don't know. The best I can say is that I feel a need to be punished for my part in it. At least I think that's what it is. Do you understand?''

"As you say, I believe it's quite common among politicians. I can read, too, you know. But why are you telling me all this?''

"You're an intelligent girl, Rebecca. I'm telling you because I mean to appeal to your sense of compassion for a fellow human being. A human being with an affliction, if you will. I want to beg you—*beg you*—to keep it to yourself. I think it would kill Jodie if she found out.''

I was horrified. "Hurting Jodie is the last thing I'd want to do,'' I said. "I hope you understand that I realize the seriousness of the thing. I also wouldn't want to hurt you. You're working on some things in Sacramento that are important to me, and I don't see how your . . . affliction, as you put it, could interfere with your work. Unless there were a scandal about it, which would destroy your credibility. So why would I want to create one?''

He opened his mouth to speak, but I stopped him. "On the other hand, I am adamant that the police must be told you were at Elena's Friday night. A woman has been murdered, after all.''

"I've already told them.''

"Good. Then you needn't worry about my telling anyone. You have my word.''

"Thank God!'' He sank back against the seat and closed his eyes, like a man who has come to the end of a long and arduous task. "Thank God!" I was quite sincerely sympathetic to him, no matter how much I liked Jodie.

As we walked back to the party, though, I felt I had to have the answer to another question. "Didn't it bother you," I asked, "when we were having that conversation about prostitution with Jodie? It was excruciating for me."

"Bother me! My dear girl, my stomach felt like someone had lit a fire in it." He made a fist and struck a tree trunk. "I hate lying to her! I hate it!"

"Does it make you feel guilty?"

He sighed. "Of course. And the more guilt I feel, the more I need . . ."

He didn't finish the sentence, but I didn't need to be told. Discipline, he meant. "Bondage and discipline" it was called in underground newspaper ads.

We reentered the house and went our separate ways. I tried to have a good time, but the evening was pretty well spoiled for me.

Mickey and I managed to get away about eleven o'clock. "Your shadow's back," she said as we turned into my block.

Sure enough, the unmarked cop car was parked next to my Volvo. There was no one in it. "He must have followed us to the bridge and then turned back." I said. "Maybe they aren't allowed to go out of the jurisdiction."

"Looks like he's taking a coffee break. Probably thought you'd be out a lot later."

I got a certain amount of pleasure out of that. I was about to go in, get the money, and drive right to the Hall of Justice with it. It would be amusing to have him miss me on that particular mission.

Mickey and I said good night, and I went inside. First I made sure the money was still in the asparagus fern, then I got the telephone book and sat down on the couch to look up the number of the police department. I figured I'd get a warmer welcome if I didn't arrive unannounced.

Putting my finger on the number, I stared into space for a

minute, committing it to memory. I'm not sure now whether I heard the noise of someone stepping out of the kitchen, or caught the motion out of the corner of my eye. Maybe both. Anyhow, I knew I wasn't alone.

"Hello, Portia," said a male voice, a voice that came out of a face that missed being handsome because it was florid and a little on the mean side. The face that belonged to Frank, the man I'd met at Elena's and again at the Washington Square Bar and Grill. He was holding a gun.

CHAPTER 15

This time I did scream. At least I went through the motions, but no sound came out.

For a big man, he moved fast and well, like one of the centaurs from *Fantasia*. He was around the coffee table before I had time to close my mouth. A stifling, sweaty hand went over it, and the gun barrel connected rudely with my ribs. Being a sissy when it comes to pain, I jumped like I do when the dental hygienist hits a sensitive spot with one of those evil little scrapers.

"I expected better from you," said Frank. "Big deal lawyer and you scream like any other broad."

That made me mad, of course, so I tried to give him a smart answer. But I couldn't with that slab of beef over my mouth. He gave me another punch with the gun, and I jumped again. "No screaming, okay?" said Frank.

I nodded as well as I could, hoping it would induce him to stop smothering me. He let me go and started to sit down on the coffee table, but I stopped him. "You'll break it."

Something his mother taught him must have sunk in, because he sat down next to me instead. His eye fell on the phone book, still open at "City and County of San Francisco." Anybody knows there's only one county office open at midnight on a Sunday, so I guess he figured out what I was doing.

"Calling the police?" he asked, almost idly.

I shrugged. By that time, I'd put a couple of things to-

114

gether, and one of them was that that orangutan was there to kill me. As a matter of fact, I figured I was as good as dead, but I wasn't going to run off at the mouth for his amusement. I had to save my breath to try to talk my way out of it.

For the moment I concentrated on figuring out why he hadn't done it yet.

Then Frank answered that question for me. He put the gun away and chucked me under the chin: "You know you're real cute?" Very self-satisfied, almost purring. He reminded me of a cat tossing a mouse around just for fun, feeling its oats as a mighty hunter, relishing its victim's agony. Frank was going to play with me before he sank his teeth in. But I didn't know yet if it was going to be mental or physical torture. Dear God, I thought, am I about to be raped? Somehow it's not easy to imagine yourself dead, even though your ribs already hurt from being pummeled with a gun barrel. Rape seemed eminently more believable, and therefore scarier.

Apparently Frank hadn't made up his mind on that one, though. He curled his thick fingers around one of my breasts as if it were an apple. "Know what I'd like to do?" he said, wheedling. Again I didn't answer. But he told me anyway. In some detail. Theoretically, I don't believe in censorship, but I'm going to skip that part. It has no redeeming social importance.

Getting that stuff off his chest seemed to clear Frank's mind. It was going to be rape, all right.

He took his hand off my breast, grabbed my arm, and pulled me on top of him. I started to flail my other arm, but he had it before I could get started. I kicked, but all I hit was sofa pillows, and I wriggled like a lizard. The pressure on my arms didn't increase, and Frank showed no signs of strain. I was so busy trying to use my elbows as deadly bludgeons, I didn't notice at first that he was laughing. When I did, it made me all the madder, and I struggled twice as hard and got just as nowhere.

It wasn't anything like a cat and mouse, really. I was completely wrong about that. But have you ever seen a cat stalk a moth? He just stares at it first, unnerving the moth so it flies into a corner somewhere. Then the cat stares some more, having a swell old time, practically chuckling. Meanwhile, the moth flutters frantically, describing the same parabola over and over again, hitting its head against the sides of the corner. I don't know why it never thinks of just flying up, but it doesn't. Maybe the cat hypnotizes it. Anyway, when the cat is good and bored with all that silliness, it just raises one dainty paw effortlessly—so fast you'll miss it if you blink—and swings the paw down on the moth's rear end. The moth's head protrudes from underneath the paw, and the cat smiles at it. I have watched cats do this, and though they do not show their teeth, I guarantee you that they smile.

After that paw is down, of course, it's good-bye, moth; but hope springs eternal in the lepidopteran breast. It keeps right on struggling. This is about the point where Frank and I were when the telephone rang.

His hands tightened like chains on my arms. I gasped, realizing the hopelessness of the situation. It was an effort to speak, but I did it. "Let me answer it."

He just kept me in that bruising grip, not saying a word.

The phone rang five times and stopped.

Frank pushed me roughly aside and sat up. The interruption seemed to imbue him with a new sense of immediacy, as if he realized it was to his advantage to dispatch me as quickly as possible and get out of there. "Are you expecting anyone?" he asked.

I didn't want to say "no," because that would give him confidence, but on the other hand, if I said I was, he'd probably just unholster his gun and shoot without further ado. I opted for "no," which was the sad truth.

Then I started playing for time. "You're going to kill me, aren't you?" I asked. He nodded. My heart doubled its speed. "How did you get in, anyway?"

"You made it easy—by leaving a key on the doorsill."

"How about the downstairs gate?"

"I just kept ringing doorbells until some trusting soul let me in without asking who I was."

"I see. Is that a trick you learned at the police academy?"

He was leaning back on the sofa, apparently relaxed. But he was watching me. I was trying to think of some way to even the odds against me. But without much success. Without the Don Quixote sculpture, which the police had taken, I didn't see anything that might make a suitable weapon.

He answered my question. "So you know. I knew you'd find out sooner or later."

I nodded. "You realized it when you read that I'm a lawyer for HYENA. Or did you catch my act on the telly?"

He didn't answer, but I had already formed an opinion: I doubted the lummox could read. I kept at him. "I defend a lot of prostitutes, and you probably arrest a lot of them. We were bound to run into each other. And I was bound to realize you don't make nearly as many arrests as you could, right? George's girls have nothing to fear from you, do they? Or are you George?"

That was the situation as I saw it. I was about to get blown away for knowing too much, like some minor character in a movie. I didn't really know why I was copping to it all, except that I didn't want to get killed without confirming the reason why. He looked mean, but he didn't answer, and all of a sudden I started to giggle. It was like that moment at the bordello when all I could think of was, "Cheezit, the cops!" It occurred to me that he ought to say, "Cut the crap, sister."

But he didn't.

He took out the gun again and held it on me while he walked over to the left-hand asparagus fern, as he had seen me do when I came in. He fished out the bundle and threw it over to me. "Count it."

"It's all there," I said. "Just like the last time you saw it."

"What the hell are you talking about?"

"Kandi stole it from you, didn't she? And hid it before

you could get here. You got in the same way you did tonight and killed her when she wouldn't tell you—''

"How much is it?"

"Twenty-five thousand dollars."

He walked over to me and poked my ribs with the gun barrel again. I was almost getting used to it. His face had run the gamut of colors in a sunset and was now the shade of my dress.

"Where did that bundle come from?"

"I found it in the fern."

I never saw his free hand move, but I found out about it soon enough. At least I don't have a glass jaw. I didn't even stagger, even though the side of my face felt like the piano had fallen on it. "Don't mess with me, Rebecca," said someone about three counties away.

I figured out it was Frank and shook my head violently, which hurt a lot. "You don't have to hit me," I said. "I swear to God I don't know how it got there."

"Oh yes you do. And you're gonna tell me in the next three minutes. Because that's about how long it takes to drown, and you don't want to drown, do you?" He didn't wait for an answer. He used his gun hand to twist my right arm around my back, and he pushed me over to the aquarium without a wasted movement. By pulling up on my arm and digging his elbow into my back, he forced me to bend over into the aquarium.

But I'd had a hint about what was going to happen, and there was time to take a breath. So at first I didn't have to deal with a mouthful of water. Only the worst pain I'd ever felt in my life, or the two worst—one in my shoulder and the other in the wrist he was gripping.

I tried to flail out with my free arm, but I couldn't move it. It was caught between our bodies. For a little while— maybe only seconds, I don't know—I clenched my eyes shut as tightly as my teeth and concentrated on not hollering.

He was twisting my arm higher and higher up my back, and I figured it wouldn't be long before it came out of the socket. This would hurt even more, and if I hollered when it happened, my mouth would fill up with water, and this would cause my lungs to do the same, and this would cause death. I told myself that if I hadn't screamed at the sight of a dead prostitute on my rug, I could make it through a little thing like a dislocated shoulder. I clenched my teeth even harder.

And for some reason, I opened my eyes. My hair danced with the anemones, and it was rather beautiful, so I watched awhile. I don't know if my shoulder and wrist were getting numb or if I just managed to distract myself, but it didn't hurt quite so badly anymore. Perhaps I was on the verge of passing out from holding my breath.

I caught sight of something red and realized it was my dress. Outside the aquarium. With some fascination, I took in the whole scene out there: part of Frank's body, turned sideways against me, and part of mine, all red and dry, twisted against his. Those two bodies seemed about a million miles away from my aqueous quarters, which were beginning to be rather pleasant.

Some tiny part of what I laughingly call my mind was working, though. I saw that Frank and I were situated nicely for the oldest trick in the world to work. I kneed him in the groin.

I may not have a glass jaw, but Frank had a glass whatever. He fell backwards, letting go of my wrist and roaring like he was shot. The gun went flying, and so did I. Out the door and down the steps, my wicked-woman shoes clacking daintily as you please. That scream I'd been holding in came out along with half a dozen of its siblings, but I didn't even mind that I'd lost my dignity. Didn't notice, in fact. I just clacked and hollered to the bottom of the stairs and pressed the buzzer that opened the front gate. I took a moment to close the gate, hoping Frank would have to stop and figure out where the buzzer was. I heard him behind me already.

I picked up the pot of geraniums on the little stoop outside the gate and ran toward Frank's car, still screaming, and not even realizing it until people started looking out their windows. I heaved the pot through the front window of the car, got in, and picked up the microphone for his police radio. I was breathing so hard I must have sounded pretty ragged. "Help!" I shouted at about nine hundred decibels. "Two-eighty-two Green Street. This is Rebecca Schwartz. Emergency! Help!" I was thinking of saying "ten-four" next, but Frank was clutching at me through the hole that used to be his window, so I just gave it one last "Help!" The radio operator was saying something, but I didn't hear it.

Suddenly Frank disappeared from the window, and I saw that a couple of men in bathrobes were hanging on to him. A woman opened the car door and asked me if I was all right. I guess they were neighbors, but I didn't know them. I couldn't answer the woman. I got out of the car silently, wondering how a person could live with a jackhammer where her heart should be. My chest felt like little bombs were going off inside it every split second, and I could barely hear the sirens above the noise of the old pump. I think Frank may have been trying to tell my rescuers he was a police officer, but I couldn't hear that too well, either.

The woman put her arm around my waist and got me to sit down on the curb. I drew up my knees and put my head down on them until I had my equilibrium back.

When I looked up, I thought I was having a stroke or a psychedelic vision or something. Then I realized the flashing lights were outside my head. They were attached to police cars. Green Street looked like the Hall of Justice parking lot.

Apparently, every cop in town had arrived, under the impression that something had happened to a brother officer. Everybody on the block was outside. Frank was gesturing toward me and thanking the cops for coming.

I got up, perfectly calm and steady on my feet, and walked over to the knot of officers around Frank.

"I'm Rebecca Schwartz," I said. "I don't know what kind of cockamamie story this man is giving you, but—"

"Shut up," said Frank. "You're under arrest."

"I'll be goddamned. You try to solicit me for prostitution,

break into my apartment, stick a gun in my ribs, half-rape me, beat me up and try to drown me, and *I'm* under arrest?''

"I tried to solicit *you*?" said Frank. "I meet you in a whorehouse, and you give me the key to your apartment and—"

"Wait a minute, wait a minute," interposed a pink-faced cop who looked about nineteen. "I think we'd better discuss this at the Hall."

Frank ignored him. "I waited for her in her apartment, ready to make a pinch for soliciting, and she came in and went to a big plant and looked in the flowerpot. I thought that was a little strange, so I took a look and she had this big bundle of money in there. She came flying at me, so I had to subdue her."

"Officer," I said to Pink-face, "you will observe that I am approximately half his size. You will also observe brand-new bruises on my face and wrist, and it cannot escape your notice that my hair and dress are wet. Don't you people have simpler ways of subduing people?"

Pink-face looked like he wanted to cry. No cop wants to think the worst of another officer, but if I didn't look like a victim of excessive force, I'm a red-haired *shiksa*.

"Rebecca, are you all right?" said a voice that sounded familiar, but I couldn't quite place it.

"Get back," said Pink-face.

"Rob Burns of the *Chronicle*," said the voice, and I looked around in time to see him offer his press card for inspection. "Miss Schwartz is a friend of mine. Can you tell me what happened, Officer?"

"I am not authorized to make any comment at this time," said Pink-face, looking around for assistance. But the other cops had gone by now, all except his partner, who was busy talking to some of my rescuers.

"Maybe Miss Schwartz will tell me, then. Rebecca, are you okay?"

"Yeah, except that I have just been beaten up and nearly drowned by an officer of the law, two days after finding a dead woman in my living room. Other than that, everything's peachy.''

I mentioned Kandi to get a rise out of Pink-face, and it worked. Apparently he hadn't put me together with the murder yet. Practically doing a double take, he flushed pinker still and bundled me into the squad car without another word.

I waved to Rob and mouthed, ''Call me.'' Dad and Chris probably wouldn't approve, but I was mad enough to tell him everything. Pink-face got in and started the engine.

''Are we leaving without the money?'' I asked, like the good citizen I am.

''What money?''

''The $25,000 I found in my flowerpot. I was about to take it down to the Hall when that ape came at me with a gun. Shall I go get it?''

Of course he couldn't turn down an offer like that, but he couldn't let me go alone, either—or he thought he couldn't—so he had to endure the humiliation of getting out of the car and escorting me inside, while everyone watched. Once again, he suggested I change into dry clothes, but I settled for a coat; I wanted the cops to get the full effect.

Pink-face and company let Frank drive his own car back to the Hall, which made me damn mad, considering who had done what to whom.

CHAPTER 16

Inspector Ziller was tall and built. He had a good jaw, a soft, drawly voice, and eyes to make a hypnotist eat his heart out. Inspector Shipe was a sweaty, pudgy cup-of-tea with hair too dark for his skin—and not much of it at that. They good-cop-bad-copped me in a room that made the Black Hole of Calcutta look like a luxury hotel. I hoped Frank's accommodations were no better.

"All right, Miss Schwartz, let's have it," said Shipe. Ziller just smiled. "How do you know Officer Jaycocks?" he said in that soft voice.

"I met him Friday night at a bordello where he propositioned me, and I did not know his last name until now. I do not know what Officer Jaycocks was doing in such an establishment, but I can tell you that I was there to play the piano."

Ziller laughed outright. Shipe grumped.

"Detailed records of my activities that evening can be found in your traffic bureau and with Inspectors Curry and Martinez of the Homicide Squad."

"Okay, okay, we know which Rebecca Schwartz you are," said Shipe. "But look, Miss Schwartz, weren't you dressed a little unconventionally Friday night?"

"I was. I was impersonating a Marin County liberal's idea of a prostitute."

Ziller smiled again, making it look as if he didn't want to but he just couldn't help it.

"Impersonating?" asked Shipe. "Did I hear you say 'impersonating?' "

"I meant I was dressed like that."

"Well, maybe as long as you were dressed like that, you played a little game with yourself. Maybe with people who didn't know you, you just didn't say you were really a lawyer, and you let them draw their own conclusions."

I'd forgotten that part. I decided to come clean. "I did more than that, Inspector Shipe. I told Officer Jaycocks a fictitious story about how I became a prostitute. That was no doubt why he propositioned me, but the fact is, he was the one who did the soliciting."

"You're sure of that, Miss Schwartz? You're sure you didn't let that little game get out of hand a little?"

"I'm sure I did let it get out of hand. But I did not suggest an illegal transaction, nor did I give Jaycocks the key to my apartment, as I believe he has claimed. I can find twenty witnesses who will tell you that I keep an extra key on my doorsill."

"That's very dangerous, Miss Schwartz," said Ziller, ever so soothing and protective.

"I'll thank you not to be condescending," I said. "Not only did Officer Jaycocks solicit me for an act of prostitution, but he also offered me a regular job with the High-Life Escort Service, which is why he tried to kill me."

Shipe gaped. "Do you think you could go over that again, Miss Schwartz?" said Ziller.

I rummaged about in my purse, which I had picked up with the $25,000, and came up with the High-Life card. "I ran into him last night in the Washington Square Bar and Grill in front of roughly 125 witnesses, not all of whom I can name, but we can start with Jeannette von Phister, with whom I was having dinner."

"And?"

"And he gave me this card and said to call if I needed work. What you have on your hands, boys, is a crooked cop." I handed over the card.

"Miss Schwartz," said the ever-polite Ziller, "I'm gonna give it to you straight; this is kind of a lot to swallow. You, a lawyer, meet a police officer in a bordello, and he thinks you're a prostitute. Then, less than twenty-four hours later, you run into the same police officer in a trendy restaurant, and he offers you a job with an escort service.

"Now wouldn't you agree that's pretty unlikely stuff? Unlikely that a police officer wold be in a bordello. Unlikely he'd just happen to be in the same restaurant where you were the next day. Unlikely he really was recruiting for prostitution. And unlikely he showed up at your house if you didn't invite him."

"Yes, now that you mention it."

"Well, how do you explain it?"

"I would have thought explaining it was your department, Inspector, but let me give it a try. You may not like to think so, but it doesn't seem at all unlikely to me that he was getting paid off to see that the High-Life girls didn't get busted, and it's just a step from there to picking up a little extra change by recruiting more women. Besides, maybe he liked that part of it. Maybe he actually owns a chunk of the business. Once you accept that, it gives you a reason for his being at the bordello—looking over the competition, maybe, or maybe scouting out talent for his own show. In fact, subsequent events bear out that possibility. Another possible explanation is that he was there on his appointed rounds as a police officer. He got a tip about the party and went investigating. Or a combination of the two: he was investigating for you people and working for George, too."

"Who's George?"

"According to Jeannette, he's the guy who runs the High-Life service. She doesn't know his last name and thinks George may be a pseudonym anyway. Shall I go on?"

"Please do," said Ziller.

"Well, there's also the possibility he showed up at the bordello for some reason having to do with Kandi Phillips, who once worked for the High-Life service, and that he followed her to my apartment and killed her."

I gave them a moment to chew on that, and then I continued with the rest of Ziller's question.

"Okay now, about that meeting at the restaurant yesterday. I didn't think about it at the time, but I looked very different then from the way I looked the night before. I don't think someone I'd met casually for five minutes would have recognized me, unless he'd expected me and known I'd be with Jeannette von Phister. Another thing—Jaycocks didn't approach me until Jeannette went to the ladies' room, which makes me think he might have been watching and waiting till he could get me alone."

"You mean he went there deliberately to see you."

I shrugged. "He said 'I've been looking for someone like you.' I don't get it either, considering I'm just an average-attractive workaday woman, but I did notice at Elena's that each of the prostitutes was a different type; I mean, each one made an attempt to cater to a different kind of fantasy. It could be that whatever meager attributes I have just weren't represented at the High-Life service."

I don't mind telling you that this speech made me pretty uncomfortable, but I said it because I thought it was true—I still do, though I must admit there is no accounting for taste in matters of sex.

Shipe lit a cigarette and blew the smoke rather artfully, so that it didn't seem it was aimed for my face, but that's where it went. He let his glance stray over my disheveled person contemptuously, letting me know what a preposterous idea I'd just proposed.

"Why didn't he just call you up?" he asked finally.

"He didn't know who I was, which is why he tried to kill me."

"We'll get to that. Suppose you tell me now how he knew where to find you, and when and with whom."

"Jeannette reconfirmed the date at the bordello the night before. He must have overheard us."

"Pretty farfetched."

"Look, I saw him standing within earshot. The man is a policeman, presumably trained in eavesdropping techniques and in retaining what he hears. I can't prove he overheard us, but I *can* tell you that's the only time I ever saw him, and he showed up the next night where I said I'd be and handed me that card." I was harping on the card because it was the only tangible bit of proof I had.

"Okay," said Shipe, weary, doing his best to show me how he suffered at the hands of liars and screwballs who tried to undermine the honor of his brother officers. "Okay. Let's get to the part about—uh—trying to kill you. Why would he want to do a thing like that?"

"About a half hour after he handed me that card, Inspector, I appeared on the eleven o'clock news of every television station in this town, clearly identified as a lawyer rather than a prostitute. This morning my picture appeared on page one of the San Francisco *Examiner*. The accompanying story identified me not only as a lawyer, but also as a lawyer for HYENA—that is, a lawyer who handles the cases of prostitutes, a lawyer he was almost sure to meet on a case sometime, who might actually cross-examine him while defending some prostitute he'd busted. And if that happened, I'd know he was a cop. And I'd realize he was a crooked cop. And I'd tattle on him, and he'd be not only out of the police department, but most probably in jail. Knowing too much will get you dead in every cheap novel ever written—and apparently in real life, too." The last came out a little bitterly, a little too defensively, as I remembered how close I'd come to drowning in my own living room.

"I came home and found him pointing a gun at me," I continued quickly, "and then he slugged me, and then he tried to rape me, and then he nearly drowned me. Also, he told me he planned to kill me and why."

Ziller actually patted my hand. "You look like you've pretty well been through it, Miss Schwartz. Let's move ahead to what happened tonight. First of all, why don't you tell us about that $25,000 you brought in with you?"

"I found it in a flowerpot just before I left to go to my parents' house. I realize now I should have brought it right over here, but—"

"Damn right you should have," said Shipe.

"Well, I meant to as soon as I got home. I was looking up your phone number when that brother officer of yours stepped out of my kitchen and stuck a gun in my ribs." I gave them the details, faltering only when I got to the part about Jaycocks trying to drown me.

Shipe held up a stubby-fingered hand. "Hold it, Miss Schwartz. Let's see if I've got this right. Jaycocks was trying to get you to tell him where the money came from, right?"

I nodded.

"Let's go back to your theory that he may have murdered Miss—ah—Phillips. I presume you're assuming the money was the motive?"

I hesitated; that theory wasn't looking terrific even to me by then. "That's what I thought at the time—and what I accused him of—but I don't know; it just doesn't seem to make sense. It seems too coincidental, for one thing, that he should first try to solicit, and then try to kill, the very person in whose apartment he'd just killed someone else."

Ziller tried to be helpful again. "Stranger things have happened."

"Well, there's more. If he killed her, he knew where the money came from, and there wasn't much point in trying to find out whether I knew—I mean, assuming he'd already made up his mind to kill me, which I contend is what he was doing there. Also—I know it sounds strange considering I'm talking about a man who is no doubt an accomplished liar— but he genuinely seemed not to know what I was talking about when I accused him of the murder." I shrugged. It was the only way I knew of expressing my discomfort. "I don't think he did it."

"Did he give any indication why knowing where the money came from was so important to him?"

"No."

"Well, you're full of theories, Miss Schwartz. Don't you have one about that?"

I was getting mad. "Hell, the guy's a sadist," I snapped. "How do I know what he considered a good excuse to play torture games?"

"Well, think, Miss Schwartz."

Shipe was nearly as bad as Jaycocks. How was I supposed to know? But I'm as good a guesser as the next person.

"The only thing I can think of," I said, "is that he was trying to figure out whether it was safe to steal it."

"If he was going to kill you anyway, there wouldn't be any witnesses. Why wouldn't it be safe?"

He had a point. Presumably nobody would know he'd killed me and therefore that he'd stolen the money. Unless of course he'd told someone he planned to kill me, but that wasn't likely. Even if he were somebody's sometime hit man—George's, say—his reason for killing me was clearly personal.

Then maybe the knowledge of where the money came from could be potentially more valuable than the money itself. Perhaps he could use it for blackmail. Or to curry favor with someone. But that meant he had to have some general knowledge of what it was doing there, and he was grasping for the specifics—a few missing tiles in a mosaic he could see, but I couldn't.

Personally, I didn't think it was a bad theory, but I knew it wouldn't cut any ice with Shipe, and anyway, I didn't see why he was asking me.

"It would seem," I said, "to be your job to find out why he did it—probably by the simple expedient of asking Officer Jaycocks himself. Why ask me?"

For the first time, Shipe smiled. "Because you're an intelligent woman, Miss Schwartz. You wait here a minute. We'll be right back."

And they left, just like that. In a minute, a guy with a camera came in. "You Miss Schwartz?" he said. "Mind if I take a few pictures of those bruises?"

"I hope you've got color film."

"Wouldn't have it any other way."

Ziller and Shipe came back when he was done, looking pleased with themselves. Smiling even. What was this? Ziller patted me again, my shoulder this time, and for the first time it occurred to me his concern might be genuine. "Looks like we've got a pretty good case," he said. "By the way, you might like to know Jaycocks was at the bordello on police business—got a tip, like you said."

"Sorry we had to be so hard on you, Miss Schwartz," said Shipe. "But when the suspect is a policeman, you've got to be about five times as careful that you've got a good witness."

I was having trouble assimilating the seeming change of heart. "You mean you believe me?"

"Look, ma'am, rubber hoses are one thing, but good cops usually don't hit lady lawyers and then dunk them like doughnuts. Your appearance kind of spoke for itself; what is it you lawyers say?"

"Res ipsa loquitur."

"That's it." He looked doubly pleased with himself, now that he'd shown off his erudition. "Look, I guess it's okay to tell you now. There've been rumors about Jaycocks for a long time, and everybody knows he's a mean son of a bitch as well. This doesn't come as the greatest surprise in the world. We had to get the best story we possibly could from you, but if you think we were tough, you should have seen what Jaycocks has been going through. We just went out to see the guys who interrogated him; his story stinks."

"So what does that mean—a departmental investigation?" I didn't have much faith in those.

"It means he'll be booked for aggravated assault in a few minutes."

Well, lordy, lordy. The system wasn't worthless after all.

They sent me home in a patrol car and had an officer walk me to my door and everything.

I flung myself into a hot bath and then into bed, but that proved to be a mistake. I should have made a few phone calls first.

CHAPTER 17

I slept for about two minutes before the phone woke me up. At least that's what it seemed like, but I guess I'm exaggerating, because the sun was already coming through my eyelet curtains.

"Darling, are you all right?" said my mother. Crossly, I wondered if she possessed any other conversational gambits.

"Certainly, Mom. Why wouldn't I be?"

"Thank God." She started sobbing. Then it dawned on me what had happened: Rob Burns's story must have made the home edition of the *Chronicle*. I'd foolishly assumed it was too late for that.

"Oh God, Mom, you must have seen the paper. I had no idea it was going to be in or I'd have called you. Look, I'm perfectly all right. Really. Just a couple of bruises."

"Darling, you could have been killed." There was some truth to this, but I thought it best to play it down.

"I'm tough, Mom. You raised me to look after myself."

"Rebecca, sweetie, I'm asking you. I'm begging you. Think of your father if you won't think of yourself. If you got killed, you wouldn't even *know* about it. But your father would have a stroke. He'd be paralyzed for life. You've always been his favorite, Rebecca—"

This was pretty extreme, even for Mom, and it frightened me instead of making me angry. I was putting her through a lot.

132

"Mom, Mom, take it easy," I said. "I'm really sorry about all this. I—"

Seizing the advantage, she jumped right in. "Darling, turn the case over to your father."

"Oh, Mom, I can't. Listen, let me talk to him."

"I'm here," said Daddy. He was on the extension.

Unnecessarily, I told Mom to stay on too. I knew she'd as soon have joined HYENA as hang up.

"I haven't even seen the paper," I said. "Could somebody read it to me?"

Daddy did. According to Rob, Frank's story was that I'd solicited him for prostitution and given him my key, like he'd told Pink-face, and he'd planned to arrest me as soon as money changed hands, but I'd resisted. The piece also contained a detailed account of my story and a vivid description off my bedraggled and bruised appearance. Apparently, Rob had gotten the whole thing from the police.

But there wasn't a word in the story about the money. For some reason, the cops hadn't seen fit to mention it; probably because it knocked a big hole in their case against Parker. I told Mom and Dad about it. Also, I told them about meeting Frank at Elena's and then again at the Washington Square Bar and Grill.

"Frankly, I think he twisted my arm and pushed me in the aquarium because he was actually trying to get information," I said. "I don't really think he killed Kandi for the money—and the police must not think so, either, since they didn't book him for murder. Which means the attack had nothing to do with the case; it would have happened whether Kandi'd been killed or not. I mean, the danger came from his trying to solicit me, not my working on the case."

"He could have been trying to find out how much you knew about the money even if he were the murderer," Daddy suggested.

"No. I accused him of the murder and said I thought Kandi'd left the money there. If he actually were the murderer, he'd already gotten as much information as he needed. He didn't have to drown me.''

Daddy conceded the logic of that. ''Okay, Beck,'' he said. ''Just let me know if you need any help.''

But Mom wasn't done. ''Rebecca, darling,'' she said, ''why did you have to go to that silly bordello party in the first place? Weren't you brought up to realize the criminal element is dangerous? You of all people? Darling, I just can't understand why a nice girl like you would dress up like that and . . .'' It was the speech I'd been dreading.

''Mom, look, it was a silly thing to do, and I'm sorry. I promise I won't—''

''But darling, I don't *understand*—''

''I don't really understand it myself, Mom. Gotta go now.''

I hung up and stretched, trying out my right arm to see if it still worked. It was stiff, but the pain was bearable. I figured another hot bath would do a lot of good.

So I walked into the bathroom, squeezed the Flokati rug as usual, picked off a few feathers and, when I couldn't put it off any longer, looked at myself in the mirror. And made a vow never again to say an unkind thing about another woman's appearance.

Half the right side of my face was an arresting shade of purplish brown and twice its normal size. All the make-up at Elizabeth Arden wouldn't disguise it.

So I'd just have to be brave. I soaked for a long time, putting off going to see Parker. But it had to be done sometime; he was probably going to be charged that day and arraigned the next, unless Martinez had evolved overnight into a person of normal intelligence.

Parker'd seen the paper, so he didn't do a double take when the Bride of Frankenstein walked in. He kissed my bruises ever so gently, even the one on my right wrist left by Frank's beefy fingers. ''How do you feel?''

''Fine. The worst part was being interrogated down here.'' That wasn't strictly true, but I thought he might be able to identify with it.

"Rebecca, I'm so sorry."

"Don't go getting guilty on me, you ape. It had nothing to do with Kandi or the case or you."

I was pretty happy with the way he reacted to the thing; he was coming back to his old self: the Parker who liked me—loved me, maybe—but didn't need me for a surrogate mother.

So I said: "Let's talk about you."

"Okay. I took my polygraph."

"Good. Did you pass?"

"I don't know."

"I'll ask Martinez. But tell me something else first. How much money were you carrying the night of Elena's party?"

I watched to see if his face gave anything away. There wasn't even an eyelash flicker. "About fifty dollars. Why?"

I told him. I may not be a physiognomist, but I swear I couldn't see a thing in his face except bewilderment, then pleasure, as he realized the money could get him off the hook. He whistled. "It kind of blows the theory that I hit her in anger."

"That's my opinion. But Martinez has a lot invested in that little theory. I'm going to see him right now. With any luck, I'll have you out today. Otherwise—uh—they'll charge you today and I'll meet you here at nine o'clock tomorrow for your arraignment."

Martinez was chewing on a pencil and looking grumpy. "You look like hell," he said. I asked him what he made of the money. "We're investigating," he snapped.

"It's what the murderer was looking for, you know. It kind of argues that Parker didn't do it."

"You don't have to prove motive in a murder case. We got witnesses that saw him at the scene, and we got a print on the murder weapon."

"He told me he took his polygraph," I said, holding my breath.

"Inconclusive."

Damn! The things aren't admissible in court, but the cops love them. If Parker'd passed, Martinez probably would have been a lot more reasonable.

"He was probably nervous when he took the test."

"How do you get around the fingerprint?"

"That's something I've been meaning to ask you about. Whereabouts was that print?"

"Around the middle of the statue, I think. What difference does it make?"

"Doesn't that strike you as an awkward way to grab a club? I mean, wouldn't you grip it near the top?"

"I might. Your client apparently wouldn't."

"You're pretty determined to charge him, aren't you?"

"Damn straight."

That Martinez should see a shrink. I've never seen a man more hell-bent on self-destruction.

It would have been unladylike to stalk out, so I just made a dignified exit without another word. Then I broke the news to Parker that he was probably going to be charged.

Seething, I went back to my office and made coffee, to have something to do with my hands, since Chris was on the phone and I couldn't buttonhole her quite yet. I counted to a hundred while the coffee cooled and noticed my hand didn't shake when I picked up the cup.

Chris and I have only two tiny little rooms opening off a tiny little entryway, so I could easily hear when she hung up. I poured another cup of coffee for her, went into her office, and plunked myself down in the client's chair. "Oh, you poor peach," she said. "I didn't know you'd look *this* bad."

"Thanks. I think they're going to charge Parker."

"Oh foot." Chris is southern and prone to talk funny now and then. She wrapped spidery hands around her coffee cup and wrinkled up her face. "Well, hell, that's the least of your worries." She produced a stack of telephone messages. "Every TV and radio station in town is hot on your trail. Also a Stacy Clayton and a Rob—um—Pigball."

"Burns. He works for the *Chronicle*. And Stacy's one of Elena's partners. Did she leave a number?"

"No. Said she might drop by sometime today. Are you going to duck the reporters?"

"I don't know. Maybe I can use them."

She frowned. Chris didn't care much for my self-serving manipulation of the press, so I decided not to tell her yet about the little idea that stack of messages had given me. Rob Burns wouldn't like it either.

I changed the subject and told Chris about the money. "Maybe it's Diddleybop's," she said. "At the bordello."

"Elena? Yeah, I was going to call her first thing this morning."

Chris pulled the phone over, and I dialed. Elena must not have been a mass media addict, because she didn't seem to know about my adventure of the night before. "Do I gather from our conversation of the other day," I began after a few pleasantries, "that Kandi got half the money for her tricks and the rest went into the co-op's kitty?"

"Right. That's the way it works for everybody."

"And where is the money kept?"

"In a safe here at the house, and then in two bank accounts: a savings and a checking."

"Are you missing any?"

"No. Why?"

"Who has access to it?"

"All the co-op members, in all three places. Why?"

"None of the part-timers? I mean Kandi, specifically. Could she have gotten into the safe?"

"No way. She didn't even know where it was. But why, for Christ's sake?"

I figured I might as well tell her. If she were the murderer, she'd guess anyway. "Because Kandi hid $25,000 in my asparagus fern before she got killed. I'm trying to find out where she got it."

Elena was silent. It would be unkind to call her an acquisitive woman, but I figured if I could see her, she'd probably have dollar signs in her eyes, like old-timey comic book characters. "We never have that much in the safe, anyway," she said at last.

"Did anyone at the party complain of missing any money?"

"No."

"What about the senator? Think hard; did he say anything that hinted at it?"

"Are you kidding? Who'd bring $25,000 to a whorehouse?"

"Well, somebody must have. Who had access to his clothes besides Kandi?"

"Anybody could have. All the co-op members would have known where his clothes were, and anyone else might have slipped upstairs, found them, and patted them down. That Frank fellow, for instance."

"No. I had a little talk with him last night, and I don't think he knew about the money. He's a cop."

"Jesus."

"Read today's *Chronicle*—you might get a kick out of it. But back to the senator. Who had access to his clothes after Kandi took them to the basement?"

"Again, anybody might have. Although it isn't really likely that any of the guests would have wandered down there."

"Did you tell the senator that Kandi took his clothes to the basement?"

"No, but for Christ's sake, Rebecca, do you honestly think the senator would be dumb enough to bring $25,000 to a whorehouse?"

"No," I answered truthfully. "I don't see why anyone would."

I hung up, discouraged. Chris had her chin cupped in her hands. "No luck?"

I shook my head and stared into my coffee cup. I guess I must have done it for quite a while without realizing time was slipping by.

"Say, Rebecca—" said Chris.

Something about her tone made me look up. "Yes?"

"You seem kind of distracted. I mean I know you nearly got killed last night, and your client's about to be charged with murder, but you are exhibiting aberrant behavior. For you, the normal reaction to all that is to shut yourself up with some music, not come into my office and stare into your coffee cup like a crystal-gazer."

I sighed. She was right, and I hadn't realized it myself till then. I was trying to keep something at the edge of my consciousness and not succeeding very well. It was Uncle Walter, the only person I knew who actually had access to $25,000 and had known Kandi.

"Anything you want to tell old Chris?"

Yes, but I couldn't. That's how bad I was. I was still trying to think of an answer when the phone rang.

It was Rob Burns. "Hi, kid. How's your face?"

"Purple, thanks. I'm glad you called."

"Jaycocks has made bail."

"So? Do you think he'll come after me again?"

"Of course not. I just thought you'd want to know. Want to have lunch?"

"Sure." I was surprised how very much the idea pleased me. "I've got some things to tell you."

"Exclusively?"

"Can't. But I'll tell you first."

"No good. The electronic parasites—also known as the broadcast media—can use it right away."

"I'll make it up to you," I said. And then thought: Whoops, Rebecca, why'd you say that?

"Done. I'll pick you up at noon."

Chris was smiling when I hung up. "Whoever that was, you like him. Good. You need a new peach blossom."

"What about Parker?"

"I don't like you consorting with the criminal element."

I threw a pencil at her.

"But seriously, folks," she said, "how are we going to get him out of jail?"

"I'll tell you how. I'm going to tell every reporter in town about the money, starting with the peach blossom on the phone."

CHAPTER 18

Her fine long nose quivered at the end. Chris didn't know it, but that was something that happened when she was upset. "What good will that do?" she asked, controlling herself.

"At best, make the cops realize they've made a terrible mistake by charging my client. At worst, just embarrass them."

"It's childish, Rebecca. And possibly unprofessional."

"Maybe, but mostly you don't like it because it goes against your genteel southern grain. You can't turn me into a lady, you know."

She let her gentility show. "Fuckin' A. Do your worst."

I went back into my own office and sat back down at my big ugly oak desk. It's an odd thing about that office, by the way; nothing could be more different from my apartment. It's cozy, lined with law books and hung with photos of my family. Not my style at all, but a warm little world I love.

There was still an hour and a half before Rob would be there, so I started making phone calls. It was true I'd told Rob I'd tell him my news first, but he'd said that was no good, so I figured all bets were off.

I'd done two phone interviews and set up an afternoon taping with a TV station when Stacy arrived. This time she wasn't the little-girl fantasy she'd been at the FDO party, and she wasn't the hard-looking child who drank sherry with Elena and me. She was well dressed, nicely made up, and looked at least twenty. She knocked lightly, almost shyly, I thought, on the sill of my open office door.

"Rebecca?"

"Stacy. Chris told me you called."

"I've been calling for two days. What happened to your face?"

Involuntarily, my hand went to my bruised right cheek. I'd forgotten about it. "Sit down," I said, and she did. "You didn't happen to call shortly before midnight last night, did you?"

"I did, yes. About eleven forty-five."

"No kidding! Well, shake, pal—you saved me from a fate worse than death. Possibly from death." She took my extended hand, puzzled. I told her how the phone call had interrupted a rape in progress and then I told her what had happened to my face and asked what I could do for her.

"I'm sorry I was such a bitch the other day," she said.

"You were upset."

"Look, I think your client or lover, or whoever he is, is guilty as hell, but I've been thinking about things. I mean, there's something I ought to tell you. In the interests of justice or something." Her mouth turned up in a half sneer, but I thought she seemed embarrassed. "I lied when we talked at the bordello."

"About what?"

"I do know someone who had a motive to kill Kandi. Two people."

If I'd been a Victorian lady, I'd have called for the smelling salts. If I'd been a Buddhist, I'd have figured my Karma had just done an about-face. But I was a Jewish feminist lawyer, so I just sat there smiling and nodding, with my heart doing ninety in a residential neighborhood.

"At least, I didn't exactly lie; I sort of forgot at the time," Stacy continued. "Elena brought it up later at a co-op meeting. In fact, she specifically asked all of us not to tell you."

She showed me those sharp little teeth of hers, meaning

to be friendly I guess, but the woman simply could not smile without looking malicious. She should see a dentist.

I had so many questions it was tough to know which one to go with. I decided on something low-key. "So why are you telling me?"

"Hell, I don't know. I guess I don't see prostitution as an honorable profession with a code of ethics and all that crap. It's a living, sure, but for Christ's sake, on the off chance your client"—she sneered the word—"is innocent after all, he ought to get a break. Also, I figure I can trust you to use the names wisely."

"It's the two guys Kandi was blackmailing, isn't it?"

"We don't know for sure she was blackmailing them."

Oh God, when was she going to come to the point? I couldn't take it much longer. "I can promise to be discreet," I said. Was that me talking? That stuffy simp?

"Good. Okay then."

I waited. I even reached for a pencil and a piece of paper to scribble the names down.

"Martin Goodfellow," she said. I scribbled. "And Walter Berman." I kept scribbling, hoping Stacy wouldn't see that I wasn't writing down the second name at all, but making crazy little loops and circles to give myself something to do so I could stay in control. Because the worst had happened. My uncle Walter had just become a murder suspect.

Those loops and circles helped, though. I was bearing down so hard I broke my pencil point, but I kept my cool. "Know anything about them?" I asked casually.

She shrugged. "I've seen them a dozen times, and they look rich. That's about all."

"I appreciate your telling me this, Stacy."

"I thought I ought to. See you later—I've got a date."

And she was gone. I turned my chair to the window and looked out to think. I had to admit Elena was right about her; she wasn't a bad sort underneath that malicious smile and defensive exterior.

"Who was that?" Chris was standing in my doorway,

looking like a fashion model in a black silk blouse and slender camel skirt. Even in the state I was in, I wished I had her figure.

"Stacy. Sit down."

"Uh oh. You sound like we is in a heap o'shit."

"I'm glad you said 'we.' But it's me, really. Listen, let me pose a hypothetical ethical problem. Suppose a lawyer's lover is accused of murder and he hires her to save his pretty ass. So the lawyer tries to find out who else might have had a motive for killing the victim and, because a prostitute with a sense of civic duty shoots off her mouth, the lawyer discovers the victim was blackmailing two men."

"Go on."

"And one of the men is the lawyer's favorite uncle." I spoke fast so I could get the words out before they got stuck somewhere on the way.

Chris's nose quivered. She sprawled back in her chair. "Oh, my poor peach blossom."

"Keep it hypothetical. We Schwartzes don't like to tell family secrets."

Chris sat up, all business, like I knew she would. She could deal with a hypothesis a lot better than she could deal with a friend in trouble. With her friends, her natural inclination was to soothe any way she could, even if it meant saying what they wanted to hear when it wasn't necessarily the truth.

"The lawyer would have to decide whether she has a diddleybop."

"Conflict, yes."

She rubbed the side of her long nose with an equally long finger. If she were a man and the old tales were true, she would probably have a long penis. "At this point, I think whether she had a conflict would depend on her emotional state."

"How do you mean?"

"If she felt she had to protect her uncle at her client's expense, well, yes, she should withdraw from the case. But investigating a murder is not normally a lawyer's job, and unless she had evidence that the uncle was *actually* the murderer, and not merely a person with a, um, nadule—"

"Motive."

"—motive, she wouldn't be obligated to tell the police. In fact, her professional status would *only* be affected if that were the case—I mean if she had hard evidence—or if she *felt* she couldn't adequately represent her client."

She was right. I could see it instantly. I nodded.

"Just for the sake of interest, what *is* the hypothetical lawyer's state of mind?"

"Screw the hypothesis. I'm all right. I can do it. You know what? I love being a lawyer."

"Oh, stop dribbling all over yourself."

"I do, really. I love the way things fit together so tidily and there's a reason for everything, except you always have to weigh everything, and it's like a constant tug-of-war."

"Some say it has nothing to do with justice."

"Well, certain specific legal questions don't, of course; I mean, certain things aren't *right*, but they *are* the law, and I even like that part of it."

"So much that you're willing to give up smoking marijuana?"

"Of course not. You have to work to change bad laws, but the code we do have is so manageable and organized and—safe."

"Cozy as a flea on a cat in a feather bed," said Chris. "Want to have lunch?"

"Can't. Got a date, as Stacy would say."

"Ah, yes. Mr. Pigball of the *Chronicle*. Give him all the news that fits."

He wasn't the only one I had news for, so I got on the phone again and continued my campaign of ruthless media manipulation.

Rob was a fashionable twenty minutes late. He wore the corduroy jacket reporters seem to consider a uniform, had a bunch of daisies in one hand, and had the other arm in a sling.

"God, you're beautiful," he said, extending the daisies. "I wish they were roses. No, diamonds."

"Purple's one of my best colors," I said. "What happened to you?"

"Nothing," he said. "Voilá!" He slipped the arm out of the sling, wiggled the hand to show me it worked, and used it to take my hand and bring it to his lips.

"Hey, cut it out." I was annoyed at being fooled. "What's the point of the sling?"

"It's for you, my dear. Misery loves company."

Well, sure I laughed. Who could help it? Then I put the daisies in a vase.

"Listen, this thing you have to tell me," he said. "It's top-secret stuff, right?"

"I've already told half your brethen in the broadcast media."

"I mean we shouldn't be overheard talking about it."

"I suppose not," I said, not sure what he was getting at.

"Good, then we can't go to a restaurant. Come with me."

I did—first to get a bottle of wine, a loaf of sourdough French bread, and two kinds of pâté from Marcel and Henri on Union Street, and then to Fort Point for a picnic. Now Fort Point, you may point out, is not a picnic area, but simply a lovely spot almost directly under the Golden Gate Bridge where teenagers go to park and tourists go to look at the view. And you'd be right. But we went there to picnic. Rob's first plan was to spread things out on the hood of his car and climb up on it, but it was too windy for that. We ate in the car.

It was a gorgeous day for it. Windy, but clear and crisp, so that persons of the leisure class were out on the bay providing a show in their sailboats, and persons of other boating classes were going about their appointed rounds as well. The bridge was right above us, just to the left, and the hills of Marin were right in front of us, making a spectacular background for the folks in the water show. What with the wine and all, I got about as relaxed and content as a lawyer with a purple face, a client in jail, and an uncle in trouble can get.

I told Rob about the money, flinching a little when I got to the part about leaving it home to go to my parents' party, but he had the decency to say he'd have probably done the same thing himself.

"Do you think she was killed for the money?" he asked when I was done.

"Yes. Do you?"

"I don't see any other way to interpret it. The question is, where'd she get it and who knew she had it? Oh yeah, and who knew she was going to be at your house?"

"Well, Elena sent her there, so she knew. And Stacy Clayton, who's one of Elena's partners, rode partway over with Kandi, so she knew. But anyone could have followed her from the bordello. The police think Parker did." Mentioning Stacy made me remember something. "Say, Rob," I said on impulse, "you haven't heard of a Martin Goodfellow, have you?"

"Sure. He's a banker—friend of my publisher's. Don't tell me he's mixed up in this."

"Stacy says Kandi may have been blackmailing him."

"Oho! That explains why the *Chronicle*'s so interested in this story. Didn't you wonder how I happened to be in front of your house after Jaycocks beat you up?"

"I assumed you heard me on the police radio."

"My dear, I have better things to do at midnight than listen to the scanner. No, the night police reporter heard the broadcast, and it was thought so important that the city editor called me at home and sent me over. The whole staff knows the publisher is hot after this story. But why was Kandi supposed to be blackmailing Goodfellow?"

"He was a client, and she thought he'd pay to see that nobody found out about it. She may have blackmailed one or two others too, apparently. At least that's what Stacy and Elena think."

"Do you know their names?"

"Yes, but—no." I never have been good at lying.

"You do."

"Don't press me, Rob. There's only one, anyway."

"Okay, for now I won't press you. But let's backtrack a little. Are the blackmailees suspects in your mind?"

"Sure."

"But then where does the money come in? I mean, if a guy was giving her money, why would he kill her for money?"

"He wouldn't. It doesn't make sense. If one of the blackmailees killed her, it had to be in a fit of anger, I think. I'm reasonably sure neither of them was at the party, though I can't be positive because I don't know what Goodfellow looks like. But assuming he wasn't, that means that he—or the other one—knew she'd be at the bordello as usual on Friday night, and he waited for her to come out, intending to follow her home for some reason. But she didn't go home; she went to my house. And he saw her ring the bell, get no answer, and leave a note stuck in the mailbox. So he figured no one else would be there, and he rang the bell and got her to let him in."

'It was taking a hell of a risk."

"True, but presumably we're dealing with somebody who was about as mad—and probably afraid—as he could get, and wasn't thinking clearly. So, okay. So Kandi let him in, first hiding the money, and he had a fight with her and killed her."

"And it had nothing to do with the money?"

"Listen, so far as I am concerned officially, she was killed for that money. That's what I'm trying to use to get the police to release Parker. But if the case goes to trial, God forbid, I'll have to use everything I can to convince a jury someone other than Parker killed her. I'll have to postulate, for instance, that she got the money from blackmailee one and was killed by blackmailee two, who knew nothing about the bundle in the flowerpot."

"You're going to first argue that she was killed for the money, and that's why your house was ransacked, and then turn around and say no, actually, that wasn't the case at all?

And how are you going to do it? Put the blackmailees—assuming, by the way, Goodfellow and the other poor slob actually were blackmailed—put them on the stand? You're gibbering, Miss Schwartz.''

I felt a tear pop into each eye and then run down each cheek. He was right, of course; you can't use that kind of stuff in any court in the country.

''Hey, come on,'' said Rob in a soft voice. ''I didn't mean to cast aspersions on your professional abilities. I thought we were having a friendly discussion in which each person was permitted to speak his mind.''

''I'm sorry, Rob. It isn't that. It's just that I'm terribly upset about something, and I'm not thinking too clearly on the subject.'' The subject of Uncle Walter.

''Oh, wait a minute. I think I'm getting the hang of things—like why you wouldn't tell me who blackmailee two is. It's someone you know, isn't it?''

I nodded.

''And you're not worried about what you're going to argue in court at all. You're feeling guilty because you do think one of the blackmailees might have done it, and you're not willing to tell the police about them.''

He'd hit it on the nose, all right. More tears came, and then outright sobs. Rob pulled me close and let me cry on his shoulder. ''Okay, listen,'' he said. ''If one of the blackmailees killed her, why did he follow her home—to your house, I mean?'' I kept sobbing. ''If that's what happened, you know, he probably didn't do it in a fit of anger. He probably meant to kill her. Do you think your friend, or whoever he is, could commit premeditated murder?''

I sat up. ''No! Or any other kind.''

''Come on, now.'' He pulled out a handkerchief and began to apply it to my face. ''Come on, look; if it'll make you feel any better, I'm willing to go in with you on a little amateur detective work. I could ask some discreet questions and find out what Goodfellow was up to Friday night—if he has an alibi, I mean. If he does, you can eliminate him. If he doesn't''—he shrugged—''you can do what you like with the information. But you have to do a little work, too. Can you find out if your friend had an alibi?''

Despair swept over me like a tsunami. ''What would be the point?'' I said.

''Well, several points. One, to assuage your guilt. Two, to give you another suspect if Goodfellow is in the running. Three, to give you a chance to clear your friend in your own head.'' He stopped and spoke in a very gentle voice: ''I guess that's mostly the point. To get you to go to him and reassure yourself that he didn't do it—because you do believe he didn't do it, don't you?''

''Yes, but—'' I couldn't finish the sentence.

''But what if he did? If he did, Rebecca, I'm afraid that makes him a murderer.''

CHAPTER 19

I said I would think about Rob's proposal, which of course meant I hoped he would do his half of it even if I didn't do mine. But I knew he was right; I had to talk to Uncle Walter.

For the time being, though, I pushed the whole thing to the back of my mind, just as I'd been doing all along, and concentrated on other things. First I called the district attorney's office. Parker had been charged with the murder of Carol Phillips and was scheduled to be arraigned at nine the next morning. That depressed me so badly I called Mickey and Alan and invited them to dinner. Alan had a rehearsal, but Mickey accepted.

I still didn't feel any better.

So I devoted myself once again to my media campaign, and rather enjoyed it, I might say, except for a slight blow to my personal vanity; greater love hath no lawyer than to oblige her client by doing TV tapings with a face like a week-old eggplant.

By the time I was done, no listener or reader or viewer in the Bay Area could fail to know that a police search had overlooked $25,000 hidden in my apartment by Kandi Phillips, who was killed for the money, in my opinion, and that in spite of all that, my hapless client—Miss Phillip's devoted brother—had been charged with the murder. Eat that, Martinez!

I'd tried like crazy to keep myself from thinking about Uncle Walter, but something must have been going on in the muck underneath my skull. At some time that afternoon I must have reached a decision. Because at four o'clock, just in time to catch Uncle Walter before he left his office, I found I was headed toward it in the Volvo.

Unlike Daddy, Uncle Walter has no juries to impress, so he can be as ostentatious as he pleases. And is, to my mother's embarrassment. It seems none of the men in her life can hit middle ground in matters of taste.

Uncle Walter's office is big enough that you hardly notice his desk, which is the size of three normal ones. The carpets are about knee-deep, and he has views to put a humble Telegraph Hill dweller to shame. And telescopes he could use to spy on Mickey in Berkeley.

Now Uncle Walter is a big man, perfectly capable of filling up that office, but he wasn't doing it that Monday. His big shoulders sloped downward, giving the impression of a much smaller person.

His secretary had phoned the message that I was on my way in, but he wasn't exactly aglow with avuncular anticipation. He was sitting with his chin in his hands, staring at nothing. He didn't even get up to kiss me.

"Hello, darling," he said, but there was no life in the words. The phrase was a thud in the gloomy office.

Murder or no murder, I didn't like my own uncle behaving like that. I decided to confront it directly. "Hi, Uncle Walter," I said, almost as gloomily. "Why aren't you glad to see me?"

He reached out for one of my hands. "Darling, I'm always glad to see you. I'm just worried about you, that's all. You should see a doctor about that face."

"I'm glad that's all it is. I thought you were depressed."

He shrugged. "Emh."

"Uncle Walter, we've got to talk about some things."

His face crumpled into that hurt, panicked look I've seen on men's faces when I have disappointed them; when I have said something they didn't want to hear and they know I will say more and they would do anything to stop the words from coming. Somehow, the face becomes triangular, and still as a death mask, but it has another quality; a hunted, trapped, don't-hurt-me look. I hated seeing that look on Uncle Walter's face, and I wanted to make it go away. That look had caused me to stay with lovers I meant to leave and to do free work for clients whose cases were hopeless, but this time I knew I had to finish what I'd started.

"Uncle, I have to know. You knew Kandi, didn't you?"

"How would I know a girl like that?"

"A girl like what?"

He shrugged again. "A sweet young thing—a girl young enough to be my daughter." The papers hadn't said she was a prostitute, but Uncle Walter didn't fall into my trap.

I had another card up my sleeve, though. I spoke softly.

"Uncle Walter, the papers never said what her nickname was."

"Your mother told me."

"I don't think I ever mentioned it to Mom."

"You must have. She knew."

Playing this painful little game was not getting either of us anywhere. "Mom told me she saw Kandi here," I said. "And that isn't all, I'm afraid. One of Kandi's—um—colleagues told me she'd seen you with her. Several times. I already know, so—"

I swear to God I saw tears in his eyes. That may mean nothing to you, because you don't know him, but the idea of my uncle Walter crying is about as believable as the Lincoln Memorial standing up and reeling off the Gettysburg Address.

"Darling, do you think your uncle Walter would kill somebody in your living room?"

"Oh, Uncle Walter, I'm so sorry. Of course not." I walked around the desk to hug him, but he turned away from me. "Uncle Walter—"

"Darling, I'm late for an appointment." He raised his wrist, and again I saw the white skin where his watch should have been.

Quickly, I circled his wrist with my fingers and rubbed the white space gently. ''She stole your watch, didn't she, Uncle Walter, as proof that she knew you? And then made you give her money to keep anyone from finding out.''

He wheeled around to face me, his eyes angry now. ''No! No! I never—'' He was shouting, and I guess he suddenly realized it. ''I mean I don't know what you're talking about,'' he said in a normal voice.

If people really writhe in discomfort, I guess that's what I did. Every muscle in my body, and especially those in my face, seemed to be working at cross purposes, twitching in opposite directions.

''Oh, Uncle Walter, I hate this!'' It came out a banshee wail. ''Look, the police have probably found the watch with her things, and it's inscribed and probably has your finger-prints on it. They could—''

''Rebecca, you're too upset to talk. I'm calling your mother.'' All those twitchy muscles had finally given way, and I was actually shaking, but Uncle Walter was back in control. He picked up the phone.

''Uncle Walter, please, please—'' I was begging now, and I realized how afraid for him I actually was. ''Please tell me what you were doing Friday night.'' It came out as horrify-ingly bald and bare as that.

Uncle Walter replaced the telephone receiver. He looked at me with eyes the color of his $500 silver-gray suit, eyes that reminded me of the pacific on a winter day—cold and deep and unknowable. ''Go, Rebecca. Get out of my of-fice,'' he said in a voice that matched his eyes.

I did, fast. The man I was talking to wasn't my uncle Walter who used to buy me raspberry ice cream cones, and I wanted out of there. My throat felt tight the way it does when I want to cry but can't.

I got in the car and tried to think while I warmed it up. He was furious like I'd never seen him. Like I'd never seen any man. I should have known he was capable of that—a person doesn't get as rich and successful as Uncle Walter by buying ice cream cones for his nieces—but it was a side of him I'd never even glimpsed. Was a man who could look at me with those eyes—me, his favorite niece!—capable of murder? I think I considered it seriously for the first time then. On the other hand, I realized that an intolerable situation had risen between Uncle Walter and me. For Walter Berman, the consummate family man, to be exposed as a person who went to prostitutes must be the worst thing that had ever happened to him. And that was only half of what I'd suggested; when you practically accuse your uncle of whoring and murder, you can hardly expect him to chuck you under the chin.

Oh God, I didn't want to think about it anymore! I turned the radio to KKHI, turned it up loud, thanked my stars something I knew was on, and started driving. God knows why, but they were playing *Swan Lake*. I hate the treacly thing, but I do know it by heart. I hummed along all the way to the supermarket, and then I sat in the car and kept it up to the end. That made me feel better, but still not good enough to start thinking.

I concentrated on dinner with Mickey instead of on Uncle Walter. Ever since my Berkeley days, spaghetti has been my favorite security food, so I bought the makings for it to get me through the night. I debated whether I should tell Mickey about Uncle Walter, but I was just being silly. I knew I was going to.

When I got home, I called Rob before I even put my groceries away, hoping—I don't know what I was hoping for, maybe just that he'd say something to cheer me up.

But he didn't. He said, "Goodfellow's clean."

"How do you know?"

"Friday night he was at a fund-raiser for a politician at the Fairmont Hotel, and after that he went drinking with friends at Alexis until 1:30 A.M., whereupon he was driven home by said friends, arriving at his Hillsborough estate sometime after two. Matter cannot occupy more than one space at a time, or something like that. Ergo, he's clean."

"How'd you find that out."

"Ordinarily a reporter does not reveal his sources, but for you . . . Suffice it so to say that I am on friendly terms with one of the Goodfellow daughters."

That annoyed me. "So that's how you got your job," I said.

"Miss Schwartz! She's married to an old college buddy of mine, an event which did not occur until long after I had proved my mettle in the trenches of journalism."

"I'm sorry. I'm just in a lousy mood."

"Uh oh. You spoke to your friend?"

"Yes, but I don't want to talk about it, if you don't mind."

"I wish—oh, hell."

"What?"

"I was just thinking how much I'd like to take you out tonight and get your mind off your troubles, but, alas, duty calls. I'm on special assignment."

"What's that?"

"Can't talk about it. I'll tell you later."

I'd meant what does "special assignment" mean, but if he wanted to be mysterious, the hell with him. I put on some music and started cutting up onions and mushrooms.

The spaghetti sauce was simmering nicely when Mickey arrived. I poured us some sherry, and we watched me on the seven o'clock news. I'd already seen the six o'clock version, but when you're a show biz newcomer, you never get enough of yourself. Mickey said I did fine.

Over dinner, we rehashed my adventure of the night before pretty thoroughly. Mickey had a few theories I hadn't thought of. "Even if Jaycocks didn't kill Kandi," she postulated, "maybe he guessed she'd left the money there and he came for it."

"He hadn't searched for it."

"Maybe you surprised him before he could."

"No good. He saw us leave for Mom and Dad's. He could have searched and been gone long before we came back. There's no other explanation except that he was there to kill me."

Mickey chewed on a bit of salad, and I poured myself a third glass of wine. It was going to take at least three to broach the subject of Uncle Walter.

"What about this?" she said. "Suppose Kandi wasn't killed for the money. Suppose she stole it or collected it from someone she was blackmailing. But meanwhile the famous George decides to make good on his threat to kill her. So he hires Jaycocks to do it. Jaycocks goes to the party, follows her here, gets in the same way he got in tonight, and bashes her."

"It wasn't exactly an execution-style killing."

"That could have been deliberate—to throw the hounds off the scent."

I considered. "Not bad. But what was he doing here last night?"

"The same reason you said; you knew he worked for George, and it was only a matter of time before you found out he was a cop. It applies even better, in fact. Murder's a lot more serious charge than pimping."

"But how was I going to connect him with the murder?"

She sighed in exasperation. "Same way I did. By using the little gray cells. *He* didn't know you were too dumb to figure it out."

I was beginning to like the theory. It was at least as good as the one Martinez had about Parker. But I had to come clean. "Mickey, she had to get that money from somewhere."

"So she blackmailed somebody."

"There's some suspicion she might have been blackmailing a couple of people."

"There you are, then. What's the big deal?"

I shouldn't have had the third glass of wine after all. I lost control and let the tears come into my eyes. "Uncle Walter might have been one of them."

"Uncle Walter! Have you lost your mind?" In her agitation, she threw out an arm and knocked over her wineglass. I was momentarily so relieved I hadn't set the table with the

white tablecloth Aunt Ellen had left me that I forgot all about
Uncle Walter.

By the time I cleaned the wine up, I was composed again.

"Mickey, listen. Uncle Walter knew her. Mom saw her at
his office."

"But that can't be!"

"Would Mom lie?"

That did it. Mickey had to accept the facts. "Not about
that," she said slowly. "But how could he have known her?"

"How do you think?"

"But Uncle Walter wouldn't—wouldn't go to a prostitute;
he's still suffering from Aunt Ellen's death."

I nodded. "I know. That's what I'm clinging to to make
sense out of it. A person might try anything to get over his
grief."

She looked skeptical.

"It's the best I can do," I said.

Mickey bit her little finger a moment before she spoke.
"It wouldn't work."

"No, but he might try it."

"Wait a minute. I'm a psychology student, remember?
You wouldn't try that to forget. You'd look for a nice widow."

"But—"

"No, let me finish. Going to a prostitute might be a good
way to avoid going on with your life, of wallowing in your
grief. You could tell yourself you're such a bad person no
one would have you."

Mickey is not dumb.

"Yeah," I said. "That makes sense." I was so sorry for
Uncle Walter, I was afraid I was going to cry again.

"Have you asked Uncle Walter about it?"

"Yes. He won't talk about it."

"So you think Kandi figured out what kind of man he is—
that he'd die of humiliation if anyone found out. And that he
had enough money to pay what she wanted."

"Yes."

"But wait. Uncle Walter may be naive, but he's not stupid. Why would anyone take a prostitute's word against his?"

"You know the watch Aunt Ellen gave him about ten years ago? He isn't wearing it."

"Omigod. Kandi lifted it."

"Yes. And the police may have found it at her apartment."

"Oh dear. So they might fingerprint it. It's obviously a man's watch."

I nodded. "If they trace it to him, there's nothing we can do about it, but what if they don't? That's almost worse."

"Why?"

"Because I would then be withholding evidence that might help my client, who is also my lover, but which could incriminate my uncle."

"You aren't withholding anything."

"Legally, no. But what about morally? If Parker had any other lawyer, he or she might have found out the same thing and would certainly—"

"No other lawyer's mom saw Kandi at Uncle Walter's."

"Oh, Mickey, listen. It isn't only that. Stacy—one of Elena's partners—came to me with his name and the name of another man she suspected Kandi of blackmailing. And not only that—"

"What?"

"Oh, I don't know. Uncle Walter was like a different person when I talked to him. I saw a side of him that I—that probably none of us has ever seen."

"What are you talking about; did he threaten you or something?"

"No, nothing like that. It was just that his eyes—"

She rolled her own eyes. "His eyes, for Christ's sake!"

"I'm not kidding, Mickey. You had to be there."

"Rebecca, you are actually entertaining the notion that your own uncle is a murderer?"

I didn't say anything.

"You are!"

"I just can't get the whole thing out of my head; that's all."

I poured myself another glass of wine, but I was so gloomy I forgot to drink it. I just sat there twirling my hair around my finger. Mickey was silent, too. I guess she needed time to assimilate the news about Uncle Walter. At last, she looked at her watch. "Want to catch yourself on the eleven o'clock news?"

"May as well." I didn't want to have to think anymore.

We went back to the bedroom, turned on the TV, and stretched out on the bed. I knew I wasn't the lead story, so I didn't pay much attention until I heard the words "mob-style violence."

I stopped examining Aunt Ellen's rose satin comforter and looked up. The film showed a gurney being wheeled into a coroner's wagon. According to the anchorman, it carried the body of Frank Jaycocks, who had been gunned down "execution-style" after leaving a restaurant with his wife.

CHAPTER 20

Involuntarily, I grabbed Mickey's wrist and held it tight till the story was over. They'd moved the interview with me up to the second lead story, but Mickey and I were no longer interested in my natterings. "He must have been working for the mob," Mickey said.

"Which means George must be a mobster." I remembered what Rob Burns had told me about the Mafia moving in on prostitution, and suddenly George's death threat against Kandi carried a lot more weight. So maybe Jaycocks *had* killed Kandi. But why had he been killed?

"He knew too much," said Mickey. "The cops would have to prove he was working for George to make the assault charge stick, and the investigation might have connected him with the mob. If it was just George, the independent operator, it wouldn't be worth murder; George could just fold his tent like the Arabs. But if George's operation were part of something much bigger—"

"But shooting Jaycocks connects him with the mob."

"How're you going to prove it? Now if Frank had talked, that'd be proof. . . ."

"I see what you mean." I was getting excited. "Listen, suppose the twenty-five grand was mob money. That would explain a lot. Like why it was so much."

Mickey stopped me. "Wait a minute. You're forgetting Kandi already had bad relations with George, and hence with the postulated mob. What was she doing with $25,000 of their money?"

"Back to the same old theory. She stole it."

"Who from? Frank? Then why'd he dunk you in the aquarium?"

"Oh yeah. And anyway, as I keep pointing out myself, the mob doesn't bludgeon people to death." My head was spinning. "And the other same old objection, too—who would bring $25,000 to a whorehouse?"

"Rebecca! We've been looking at this wrong. Remember what you said when I was stoned? No one would."

"But Elena says it wasn't co-op money. So unless she's lying, someone did."

"That's what I mean about looking at it wrong. We should have been asking ourselves *why* anyone would. And once you have the answer to that, it's perfectly credible that *anyone at that party* would have had $25,000 on the premises of a whorehouse. Because he *didn't* bring it there. He picked it up there."

My head had stopped spinning and taken to pounding. "Omigod. Someone brought it there to give it to somebody else who was going to be there."

Mickey nodded, but she was frowning. "But why? Why transact business at a bordello?"

"It could have been blackmail money for Kandi. But neither Uncle Walter nor the other man was there. My head hurts."

But Mickey was on a different track. "Some kind of bribe or payoff?"

I scarcely heard her. "I'm getting a headache," I said. I got up and went to the bathroom for some aspirin.

That damn Flokati rug was still hanging over the bathtub. I forgot all about the aspirin. "Mickey!"

She was there in half a second. "What? Are you all right?"

"It was the senator."

"What was? And what senator, for that matter?"

"The murderer. Oh, Jesus, it's so clear—that sonofabitch

and his damned righteous feminist stand on legalized prostitution! I ask you, who'd benefit by legal prostitution?"

"Wait a minute! Are we unmasking a murderer or having a philosophical discussion?"

"I'll tell you who would—besides prostitutes, I mean—the mob. No messy busts, no tiresome payoffs, and probably a nice legal tax dodge for laundering illegal money. Now if the mob wanted to take over prostitution in San Francisco, wouldn't it be to their advantage if it were all nice and legal?"

"What *are* you talking about?"

"Well, it would, and the mob does. If Rob Burns is right. And they paid Senator Calvin Handley—murderer of Kandi Phillips and friend of the downtrodden prostitute—$25,000 to work on his fellow legislators."

Mickey opened her mouth and left it like that, which is an annoying habit she has on the rare occasions when she is speechless. "Look, Mickey," I said, as patiently as I could. "Handley was the mysterious client I told you about." I was still working the thing out in my head and couldn't be bothered to explain further. Mickey closed her mouth and sat down on my bathroom floor. Finally she asked, "What makes you think he was taking payoffs?"

"The feathers," I said, not realizing I was more or less dithering. "Someone at the whorehouse was a courier. Who? Elena? No, she'd never have sent him out without his clothes. And Kandi's the last person she'd have let near his stuff if she'd thought there was $25,000 in his pants pocket. Stacy! He requested Stacy specially that day."

"What the hell," asked Mickey, "are you talking about?"

"Stacy was the one who brought the money to the whorehouse. Omigod! So she must have known who the murderer was all the time. Now, why didn't he—oh Jesus, she couldn't have known because she didn't know where the money was. No one except the senator would know Kandi had taken it. But after I shot off my mouth on TV, everybody would know." I paused as I realized what it meant. "The senator would know that Stacy would know."

Mickey walked back into the living room and sat down, shaking her head. I knew it was confusing, but I couldn't stop to explain. As long as the old brain was in gear, I didn't want to jar it. Besides, I didn't think I had any time to waste. I joined Mickey in the living room, called directory assistance, and asked for Stacy's number. She wasn't listed. So I called Elena and got a busy signal.

So I called the cops and asked for Martinez, who wasn't there. Finally I got Ziller, and I think I said something like this: "Hi, it's Rebecca Schwartz, you've got to put a guard on Stacy, the senator's going to kill her."

"Nice to hear from you, Miss Schwartz," said Ziller. "Do you think you could go over that again?" He really was a sweetheart.

So I explained to him that I had deduced that one of California's most respected state senators had accepted a payoff from the Mafia, killed a prostitute, and now was about to kill another prostitute because she had probably figured out that he'd committed the first murder. He may have already told the police he was at the bordello the night of Kandi's murder, I said, and there might be a record of that.

Ziller said he would look into it, and did I have any other proof?

No, I said, but any fool could see . . .

"Well, we'll look into it, Miss Schwartz," Ziller said.

"But Stacy may be in danger right now," I said.

"Then again, she might not be," Ziller said in a voice that indicated he wasn't going to humor me much longer, and that the San Francisco police couldn't go around acting on no evidence at all, especially where state senators were concerned.

I thanked him for his trouble and rang off, getting more agitated by the second. I dialed Elena again and got another busy signal. I dialed the operator, told her I had an emergency, and asked her to break in on the conversation. But there wasn't conversation; Elena had left the phone off the hook, which was something I knew she did every now and then when she wanted a little peace.

It's a tribute to Mickey's faith in me that she hadn't run screaming from the room by this time. She'd just sat there looking expectant and chewing her cuticle. She didn't even protest when I said we had to get to Elena's right then, no time to waste.

She didn't till we were in the car, anyway. As soon as I had the Volvo's nose pointed toward Pacific Heights, she said, "Now. What is the purpose of this wild-good chase?"

"What do you mean?" I didn't understand what she didn't understand. "We have to find out where Stacy is. To warn her."

"I've got the basics," she said. "I mean, I know you think Calvin Handley killed Kandi and might kill Stacy, but what I want to know is what in God's name gave you that idea?"

"Oh. The feathers."

She nearly lunged at me, but I held up my hand to let her know that if she would control herself, I would tell all. And I did:

"When I saw the Flokati rug in the bathroom, I remembered how Kandi's dress had been shedding feathers Friday night. Now Elena had told me that Kandi took the senator's clothes back down to the basement that night, and that he later called for them. So that came back to me when I saw my rug with the feathers all over it, and I realized that she couldn't have handled his clothes without getting feathers on them."

"And," finished Mickey, "that if he'd happened to miss $25,000 from his pants pocket, he'd deduce that she stole it."

"Right. And if he were the one with the money, it would explain why he'd been so insistent about going back to the bordello even though he thought it was crawling with cops. I missed that before because I eliminated him as the one with the money, because (a) he didn't have that kind of money, and (b) he wouldn't bring it to a cathouse.

"Once we got the idea that someone brought the money there to give it to someone else, and I got the idea the recipient was the senator, I naturally started thinking about why. And came up with the idea of a payoff from the mob to push legal prostitution. If that were the case, then who was the courier?

"Elena told me his routine had been completely different that Friday—for one thing, he'd come in the afternoon, and for another, he'd especially requested Stacy as well as Kandi. Ergo, Stacy must have been the courier."

"Aha!" said Mickey. "And until tonight Stacy couldn't have known Kandi was killed for the money, because she assumed the senator still had it. But after you told the whole world that $25,000 had turned up in your apartment, Stacy was bound to hear about it, put two and two together, and become dangerous to old Calvin. Hence this wild-goose chase."

"You catch on fast, kid."

Elena's porch light was on, and it wasn't red. Anybody could have seen us get out of the car and walk up to the door. I realized someone had when I heard light footsteps running across Elena's tiny garden from the right side of the house. Mickey gasped. I wheeled around, clutching my purse like a weapon, ready to wrangle with a seven-foot plug-ugly. But the figure coming at us was slender and barely five-feet-ten. It was nattily attired in jeans and a corduroy jacket, and it was stage-whispering my name. It stopped in midyard and beckoned us over to it.

"It's all right," I told Mickey. "It's only a reporter on special assignment—Rob Burns, the *Chron*'s illicit-sex expert."

Rob put a finger to his lips as we joined him. I introduced Mickey. "You're not going to believe who's in there," Rob said, hardly able to contain his delight.

"The senator!" Mickey mouthed, and her face was so genuinely horrified that Rob sobered up.

"You know?" he said.

"Calvin Handley's in there?"

Rob nodded.

"Let's go." I turned and started grimly back to the porch. But Rob grabbed my arm.

"No. Listen, there's a place on the side of the house where the drapes don't quite meet. Mickey and I could boost you up high enough so you could look in—and maybe hear what he and Elena are talking about."

"Is that the way reporters normally work?"

He had the grace to look sheepish. "Of course not. But dammit, Rebecca, you don't know what I know. He's up to something pretty sleazy."

"Damn straight," I said. "Lead on, MacDuff."

When I had one foot in each of their clasped hands, with the wall of the house for support, I could just see in the crack. Elena and the senator were sitting on the rose velvet loveseat, and the crucial moment seemed to have arrived.

"But you didn't come here to find out how I'm getting along," Elena said, or something quite close to it; I could catch most of the words. "You must have a pretty compelling reason to take this kind of risk." Her eyes were shrewd.

"You're an astute observer, Elena. I wouldn't have come unless it were a life-or-death matter. Stacy may be in danger."

"What sort?"

"I can't talk about it, or tell you how I got the information, but I want to warn her."

"And you want me to deliver that message?" Elena looked puzzled.

"No, no—there's a specific message, and I—well—to tell you might endanger you as well. I must talk to her myself."

Elena shrugged. "I can give you her address and phone number, but I sent her out on a dinner date, and she won't be home for hours."

"Uh—forgive my ignorance, but how does a dinner date work?"

"Just like the amateur kind, only the guy pays for the pleasure of your company. Mostly guys from out of town. They want to take a good-looking woman to an expensive restaurant like Amelio's, which is where I sent Stacy, and they want to make damn sure the evening's going to end up with sex."

"At his hotel?"

"Usually, yes."

"And does the woman stay all night?"

"If the john pays for it. This guy didn't, so Stacy ought to be home by about one o'clock at the latest."

I'd heard enough. I told Rob and Mickey to let me down.

Rob was so excited he was practically doing a jig. "What's going on in there?"

"That man is going to commit a murder tonight, unless we stop him," I said. "Rob, you wait for him to leave and then bang on the door until Elena answers. Tell her to call Stacy immediately and tell her I'm on my way to get her at Amelio's. Tell her to tell Stacy to get rid of the john and come with me, and not to leave under any circumstances until I get there."

"What? Are you crazy? I'm supposed to be following the senator. Also, I haven't a clue who Stacy is or what any of that means."

"It's an emergency, dammit. Come on, Mickey."

But she balked. "Don't you think we should call the cops?"

"I'm damned if I'm going to make a fool of myself again. We'll just pick up Miss Stacy Clayton and take her to the nearest cop shop, which I believe is Central Station. Why don't you meet us there, Rob, and I'll explain everything? No time now."

"Fuck!" said Rob Burns of the *Chronicle*.

I had in mind to leave with a great screeching of tires, but the Volvo stalled. It is an eccentric car and does this some-times.

It took about five minutes to get the damn thing started, and I kept telling myself I wasn't worried. I trusted Rob to deliver the message and Elena to be forceful enough to con-vince Stacy of the urgency of the situation and Stacy to be smart enough to wait for me and the senator to be canny enough to go immediately to Stacy's and start booby-trapping her house or something. It would hardly serve his purpose—which was keeping her quiet—to hie his Mercedes over to Amelio's and march in and gun her down.

As I said, that's what I was telling myself. But the urgency to get there was almost unbearable. What if Stacy left the restaurant before Elena could call? What if Rob decided I was crazy and carried out his assignment of following the senator and didn't even deliver the message? Oh God, what if the Volvo just plain gave up?

I heard a car start in the alley behind Elena's.

"That must be the senator," said Mickey in a controlled voice. "Let's try it again."

I shifted and the Volvo started, and we did great for four blocks until we hit a red light at Fillmore.

"God damn it!" I said. "Dammit, dammit, dammit!"

"Easy, girl," said Mickey, who apparently had appointed herself my caretaker. "The thing I don't get—"

The Volvo screeched forward again, faster than it should have with an officer of the court at the wheel, but Mickey kept on talking, either in a frantic effort to get me interested in something besides killing us both or in blind ignorance of the danger she was in; it couldn't have been faith in my driv-ing. "The thing I don't get—"

"Christ on a crutch!" Some idiot was stopped in my lane, talking to someone on the sidewalk. I leaned on my horn. He didn't budge. I kept going, and Mickey covered her head with her hands.

At the last second, I had to swing into the left lane to go

around him, no matter if there was an oncoming car. There was. His brakes screeched. So did mine.

We both stopped in time, but it was a good thing Mickey and I had our seatbelts on, or we'd have ejected like a couple of refugees from a James Bond movie.

The other driver—a large and angry-looking black man—got out of his car and came forward, no doubt with the intention of giving me a well-deserved piece of his mind, or possibly a rap in the teeth. I leaned on my horn.

"What you think you doin', bitch?" he shouted over the din.

"My sister's having a baby," I shouted back, still honking. Mickey cowered in the shotgun seat.

"I don't care if she's havin' a epileptic fit. You oughta know better—"

"*Now*, Rebecca!" shouted Mickey.

The car in the right lane had taken the hint and left rubber all over the street. I swung back into that lane and followed suit, fighting down the urge to give the other driver the finger. Sure, he was a jerk who'd have let Mickey give birth right in the Volvo, but after all, the whole thing *was* my fault.

It was a good thing I let him off, too, because I hit another red light at the corner, and he could have caught up with us and killed us if he'd wanted to. I swore and Mickey kept cowering until we got on the freeway at Gough Street and I got in the fast lane and gunned that little gray mother, a good fifteen minutes from takeoff.

Amelio's was in North Beach, nestled on Powell Street, just south of Washington Square. The senator could have already been there if he'd had any better luck than we had. But he wouldn't be, I told myself. What was the point?

"What I don't understand," said Mickey, "is how he can kill Stacy now that Elena knows he was asking about her. I mean, doesn't he have to kill her to cover his tracks?"

I'd thought of that too. "He's not going to get the chance," I said. "He doesn't know we know what he's up to, and if

Stacy gets it, I've got an idea the police will listen to me for once."

"Yes, but unless he's gone completely mad, surely he wouldn't take the risk. It doesn't make sense, Rebecca. And neither does the other part, really. He's always been a decent politician. Unless he's in some terrible financial difficulty, why would he sell out to the mob?"

"Dammit, Mickey, he was at Elena's with a cockamamie story, wasn't he? What kind of proof do you want?"

"I don't say you're wrong," she said in a hurt voice. "I just don't understand *why*, that's all."

"Power corrupts," I snapped, aware that it was a facile answer, but I was tired out from thinking too much. I'd have to worry about that part later.

Mickey didn't answer, and we were silent as we fetched up at the Broadway exit and began fighting our way through the North Beach traffic. It was much too slow going for my peace of mind, so I turned right on Sansome and went to Union, so as to approach from the north. We turned off Union Street onto Powell, and I pulled up kitty-corner to the restaurant. I couldn't get directly across the street because of the parking garage there that's always debouching cars at unsafe speeds, but it didn't matter; we had a clear view of Amelio's. Stacy wasn't outside.

"I'll have to go in and get her," I said. "Take the wheel, and be ready to scratch off when we come out."

"We're in that big a hurry?"

I nodded. "I think so, yes."

"I'm not sure I can handle your car." She had a point. When the Volvo gets temperamental, no one but me can figure out how to coax it into submission. "Okay, you go," I said.

"But she doesn't know me. Elena told her to wait for *you*, remember?"

"Dammit, yes. Here—take my driver's license for proof you're with me." I fumbled for it and described Stacy briefly.

"If she has any doubts, just have her peek out the door and I'll wave."

"Okay." She darted across the street, slender and lithe in her jeans.

I waited about five minutes, clenching my teeth and every now and then taking my hands off the steering wheel and wiping them on my pants. I also kept glancing at my watch, which is how I know how long I waited. I don't have to tell you how long it felt like.

Mickey and Stacy came out looking like a couple of old-fashioned butch-femme lesbians having a lover's quarrel, the way they were dressed—Stacy was in some sort of floaty white dress—and the way Mickey was practically dragging her kicking and screaming. Stacy looked briefly my way, and I waved as promised, but that didn't seem to relieve her mind any. Apparently, the problem wasn't whether the right person was calling for her; she didn't seem to want to be called for at all. I figured it had something to do with the hundred bucks she stood to lose by cutting the date short and shifted into drive as they started across the street.

As I glanced back up from the gearshift, a Mercedes whipped out of the parking lot, heading right for them.

I made no decision, or if I did, I don't remember it. All I remember is stomping the accelerator flush with the floor, and then a godawful crunch as I hit the Mercedes broadside.

I couldn't see if the driver was the senator, or if Mickey and Stacy were safe. I don't remember seeing anything at all. All I really know about what happened next was that someone lost her cool and screamed. The way I knew it was me was I noticed my mouth had filled up with glass.

CHAPTER 21

I won't keep you in suspense; I wasn't killed. Neither was anybody else. But I did spend the second longest night of my life lying on a gurney at San Francisco General Hospital, also known as Mission Emergency. I don't remember getting there, so I can't tell you what that was like. I just remember feeling I was going to throw up, which is how concussion sometimes affects you, and holding Mickey's hand.

I managed to break the senator's hip, which I am not the least bit sorry about to this day. The sonofabitch would have killed my sister if I hadn't rammed him. He got most of the attention in the emergency room, and I vaguely remember Jodie Handley coming in at some point. Mom and Dad didn't, because Mickey and I decided not to call them till we got back to my house. As it turned out, that was around daylight.

Mickey made breakfast and brought it to me, and we both got under Aunt Ellen's satin comforter to eat it. I felt a lot better after a couple of poached eggs on toast, but not well enough to call the folks.

Mickey did, and laid it on so thick about how I'd saved her life that they were scarcely any trouble at all. Mom did say she'd be over later with soup, but I suppose that was inevitable. Dad just kept repeating Calvin Handley's name in disbelief.

They were so grateful about my saving Mickey that I decided I was a heroine and called Chris with quite a spirited version, heavy on grisly details but light on explanations. Unfortunately, I still needed some.

Then I got a call myself—from a steaming Rob Burns wanting to know why I hadn't turned up at Central Station. Imagine the fun I had with that one! In the course of it, I also learned that he'd heard about the senator's mob connections from "sources," which is why he was carrying on like some character from the Lou Grant show the night before. He never has named the sources, though—either to me or to the police.

By then I was a big fan of Rob's, but I could hardly wait to get him off the phone, which wasn't easy considering he'd stumbled on a page-one story. Of course, in a couple of hours he could have gotten it from the cops, but then so could any other reporter, and he'd sewed it up for himself just by dialing my number.

Anyway, the reason I was so eager to get rid of him was I wanted to call Martinez. I wanted to relish informing him from my bed of pain how his cockamamie theory about Parker had nearly caused two more murders, including that of my own sister, and how I had risked my life to straighten out his botched investigation and how if he didn't let Parker loose in the next five minutes, I'd have his job.

But it wasn't any fun at all. It seems Jodie Handley had had a heart-to-heart with her hubby, and she'd called Martinez at home. Even as we talked, Martinez gave me to understand that my client was being released. Somehow he managed to convey that he'd solved the case himself, and he didn't say he was sorry or ask how my head was, the horse's ass.

I stayed in bed that day and the next, and Mom came, and so did Chris and Rob and a lot of other reporters, but I had Mom send them all away but Rob.

Parker came too, with a couple dozen roses, but he didn't stay long. We were distant with each other, somehow, and we both knew the romance was over; the time just wasn't right for it.

The person I was happiest to see was Uncle Walter. He took my hand and 'fessed up and said he was sorry for the way he'd treated me. I said I was sorry for what I'd done too—suspecting him of murder and all—and we got back on solid uncle-niece ground again. Kandi'd tried to blackmail him, all right, but he hadn't given her a cent. I'm proud of him. And I'm happy to say the police found his watch and gave it back.

The senator pleaded guilty to second-degree murder and a few lesser charges. I was exactly right about what happened:

He'd panhandled a dime after he left me, called Elena, and gone back to the bordello to find his clothes with Kandi's apricot feathers on them and the money missing. Then he'd gone out the back door again, retrieved his car, and waited for Kandi at the front of the house. When she came out with Stacy, he saw he couldn't accost her on the street, so he followed her to my apartment. She went in immediately, leaving the note for me, and he rang my bell. She let him in, apparently stashing the money in the fern pot while he mounted the stairs. She told him she didn't have it, they quarreled, and he lost his temper and hit her with the statue, holding it by the head as I'd postulated. He took out his handkerchief and wiped it immediately, unknowingly leaving Parker's print on it. Then he went into the kitchen and found my rubber gloves to wear while he looked for the money.

He lied to Elena and me about telling the police he was at the bordello the night of the murder.

When I told every reporter in town I'd found $25,000 in my apartment, he assumed Stacy would hear about it and realize that Kandi had stolen the money from him and that he'd killed her to get it back. So he tried to kill Stacy before she could talk. He'd thought that if he made it look like an accident, Elena either wouldn't put two and two together or would find it to her advantage not to mention his interview with her at the bordello. After all, she wanted prostitution legalized, and he was a state senator working on that project—as well as a good customer. He counted on her being just enough outside the law to take that attitude and just straight enough not to try to blackmail him.

At least that's what he told Jodie. But I say a person who's committed two murders probably wouldn't stop there if he thought there were any doubt about his own neck.

Jodie got the job as lobbyist for HYENA, and we had lunch not too long ago. She told me she'd filed for divorce, which I believe is the right thing to do when someone breaks your heart. She also described—fairly painfully for both of us—the deterioration of a once-decent man. It had to do with the same things the senator was telling me about at Mom and Dad's party—about making compromises and so many things in politics being about half-crooked anyway. He'd just kind of gotten jaded after years of being forced to make this or that compromise or deal to get his bills through, and his integrity had begun slowly to crumble. Jodie had seen it and worried about it, but she had had no idea how far it had gone. When he'd gotten the offer from the mob, it hadn't seemed such a bad thing; after all, they were asking him to do something his wife was already pressuring him about, something she thought right and moral. Why not do it and get something out of it as well? It was a kind of self-destructive game, a kind of weary giving in to his worst side almost as a sort of self-punishment, like those games he'd played with Kandi. He just took up legislative residence in Edge City.

But he hadn't become so grasping and corrupt that he'd kill someone for money. After he'd played his nasty little game with the mob, the payoff did assume a great deal more importance in his mind than his actual need for it, so he confronted Kandi about it. But he killed her because she taunted him. She called him a sicko and a weirdo and a crook who made her want to throw up. It wasn't exactly an insult Dorothy Parker would have been proud of, but it was effective on two counts: it was exactly his opinion of himself, and it came out of Kandi's mouth. Before that, he'd thought of

Kandi as some sort of mechanical doll—not even a real person, never mind a worthy one—and here she was setting herself up as *his* superior.

He told Jodie that in retrospect he believed he had turned his own guilt and self-hatred on Kandi for the split second it took to bash her head in, and I expect that's not far from the truth.

Jodie's bounced back pretty well, and I'm going to introduce her to Uncle Walter at the first opportunity; I think they just might hit it off.

Stacy got immunity for telling a grand jury who it was she'd delivered the money for, and a whole string of indictments followed for various offenses, including the murder of Frank Jaycocks. None of the indicted men was named George, but I always thought that was a pseudonym.

Elena the incorrigible found herself a new house and went right back into business. If she gets busted again, I don't know what I can do for her, I'm so swamped with clients. I'm almost as big a name as Daddy now, but I haven't let it go to my head. I'll make time for Elena if I have to; don't worry.

The police gave back my Don Quixote statue, but I couldn't bear the sight of it anymore, so I gave it to Rob Burns for a souvenir. He and I are quite a heavy number now. In fact, he promised to give me something to replace the statue, and I know exactly what I want: one of those heart-shaped red ceramic boxes you can get at a gift shop on Polk Street for about twenty dollars. They only sell them around Valentine's Day, but I can wait.

About the Author

Julie Smith is the author of eight mysteries, including *New Orleans Mourning*, which won the 1990 Edgar Award for Best Mystery Novel. A former reporter for the New Orleans *Times-Picayune*, the author lived for a long time in San Francisco and currently makes her home in Berkeley, California.